The
UNIMPLEMENTED
OVERLORDS
Have Joined the Party!

Wow! If fetch quests are this easy, I won't bother with other quest types anymore!

Player:

MISAKI

A newbie gamer just finding her footing in the game world.

"How did you get here—?"

"Oh... What are we going to do?! We can't— We can't log out!"

Player:
SHUUTAROU
A middle schooler playtesting *Eternity*. Got teleported to an unexpected location after using his Create Dungeon skill.

Boss Mob:
VAMPY
The Second Evil Overlord. Takes an interest in Shuutarou, who somehow doesn't die when he touches her.

"Do not give in to despair! My guild, Crest, will share with you everything we know about the game's mechanics, design, and survival skills!"

Player:
WATARU
The leader of Crest, a guild with a huge membership.

"The title of Evil Overlord indicates the leader of a wicked race... and the three of us here are rulers of our respective races. Therefore, we are all Evil Overlords."

"What I mean is, if you're Evil Overlords, why'd you put me on your throne?"

"Simple. You are our master, and as such, this throne belongs to you."

ELROAD

The First Evil Overlord. Always calm and composed.

THEODORE

The Fifth Evil Overlord. A warrior who crafts his own weapons and armor.

The UNIMPLEMENTED OVERLORDS Have Joined the Party!

1

Nagawasabi64

Illustration by Kawaku

YEN ON

NEW YORK

The UNIMPLEMENTED OVERLORDS I Have Joined the Party!

1

Nagawasabi64

Translation by Kiki Piatkowska
Cover art by Kawaku

MIJISSO NO LASTBOSS TACHIGA NAKAMA NI NARIMASHITA.
Vol.1
©Nagawasabi64 2020
First published in Japan in 2020 by KADOKAWA CORPORATION, Tokyo.
English translation rights arranged with KADOKAWA CORPORATION, Tokyo through TUTTLE-MORI AGENCY, INC., Tokyo.

Yen On
150 West 30th Street, 19th Floor
New York, NY 10001

Visit us at yenpress.com • facebook.com/yenpress • twitter.com/yenpress • yenpress.tumblr.com • instagram.com/yenpress

First Yen On Edition: February 2024
Edited by Yen On Editorial: Rachel Mimms
Designed by Yen Press Design: Eddy Mingki

Yen On is an imprint of Yen Press, LLC.
The Yen On name and logo are trademarks of Yen Press, LLC.

The publisher is not responsible for websites (or their content) that are not owned by the publisher.

Library of Congress Cataloging-in-Publication Data is available.

ISBNs: 978-1-9753-7117-3 (paperback)
978-1-9753-7118-0 (ebook)

1 3 5 7 9 10 8 6 4 2

LBK

Printed in the United States of America

1

Nagawasabi64

Illustration by Kawaku

CON

START
DEATH GAME »

Contract: { Boss Mob }
The Six Evil Overlords
and the Dungeon Master

T E N T S

Activation 〈 Create Dungeon 〉

《 VRMMORPG 》 Eternity 》

One boy was finishing creating his game character. The last thing to do was to generate a random skill. The one he got was called Create Dungeon.

"Hmm… Sounds fun! I'll go with that!"

He confirmed it without a second thought.

The boy named Shuutarou had no idea if the skill was any good. It wasn't listed on the game's wiki page, but lots of skills weren't. And that wasn't due to some oversight or lack of interest in the game.

Eternity had been in closed beta for the past month, so it had only been played by a hundred playtesters so far. But it wasn't the only reason. The Mother AI, which governed the game's mechanics, could generate practically an infinite number of skills, or so the devs claimed.

There was a fade-out effect before his surroundings got bright again, and Shuutarou saw he was in a town with buildings made of stone. The setting was based on medieval Europe, as was common for fantasy games—and there were so many people.

"Battles first, making friends later!"

Under the clear blue sky, Shuutarou set off running to explore the world of this game, which had been named for its supposedly endless possibilities.

*   *   *   *

A major Japanese video game studio had only recently announced the release of *Eternity*, a brand-new, cutting-edge VRMMORPG priced at two hundred thousand yen and first released domestically.

The VR and AI technology were top-of-the-line, and the game was a true showpiece for the latest possibilities of VR entertainment. But the price attracted criticism, mostly from students and homemakers. Then another announcement came.

A hundred people would be chosen at random from the applicants to beta test the game for free. Of course, the chances of being among the chosen one hundred were astronomically small, and most of the hopeful candidates ended up in tears when they didn't make the cut, Shuutarou included.

Gameplay videos from the beta testers and *Eternity* ad campaigns generated a lot of buzz for the game, and the increased interest prompted the developers to announce that a hundred thousand people would get to play for free from the day of the official release.

Many potential players got on the waiting list, but their chances of getting picked were much better this time around. Shuutarou was lucky enough to be among those hundred thousand people.

The official release took place a month after the beta. On launch day, *Eternity*'s population—the hundred beta testers, the hundred thousand free players, and those who had to fork over the money to buy the game—numbered three hundred fifty thousand.

*   *   *   *

Shuutarou made quick work of the first enemies he encountered before sitting under a tree for a short break.

"It's just rats! Surround them!"

"It bit me! I'll make it pay!"

"Don't hit it with your staff! Use magic! Cast spells!"

A group of three players was struggling against a low-level rat monster.

Monster: Demi-Rat	Level 2

These were the weakest rat monsters in the area, but *Eternity* was a novel VR game, where everything seemed real, present, and immediate. It wasn't anything like its predecessors. Even with full LP (life points) and MP (mind points), every single battle, minor as it might be, felt as risky as if your life was at stake; there was this sense that it was real, you were there, and your stamina was being chipped away at.

"I'm gonna use my special!" a boy with a sword cried out.

His weapon flashed, sending a shock wave at the rats, which were knocked up into the air. They glowed faintly, after which they shattered into polygon shards. The boy's party cheered.

Unique skills were a big selling point of this game.

Everyone got one randomly generated unique skill at the end of character creation. These bonuses from the Mother AI weren't part of any class skill set, but they often had good synergy with the player's class or their weapon of choice. Sometimes, they were completely unrelated.

Shuutarou wasn't particularly impressed by the boy's showy skill. He opened his status window and navigated to his own unique skill.

Create Dungeon: Creates a dungeon under the present location. Small chance of obtaining treasure upon activation.

Just like the other player, Shuutarou had picked swordfighter as his character class, and his weapon was a sword—popular choices among boys his age. But his unique skill was very different from what the rat-slayer had.

Let's try it out and see what it's like.

Seeing it in action should make its worth obvious.

Shuutarou placed one hand on the ground, ready to activate the skill. He was looking at his status screen, so he didn't notice the blue sky suddenly turning an ominous purple.

"Create Dungeon!"

There was a bright flash accompanied by a deep rumble. Shuutarou disappeared, swallowed up by the ground underfoot.

* * * *

Meanwhile, the clouds parted over the city of Allistras, the spawning point for new players, revealing a giant wyvern. Menu screens opened for all players, including the party of three who had just defeated the rat monster.

"What the heck? It's in the way."

Another demi-rat spawned nearby and pounced at the boy complaining about the devs messing with people's menus.

"Watch out, Jun! A rat!"

The party member who warned him was smiling, not very concerned about the rat. The boy wasn't scared, either. A rat attacked him earlier, and it didn't do much damage.

The rat bared its large incisors and bit the boy's shoulder.

"Owwwww! This hurts! What the heck?!"

His sword slipped out of his hand, and he fell to the ground. The rat wasn't letting go, and the boy kept screaming.

"Jun?! Are you faking it? It can't really hurt, right?"

"Stop it already. You're attracting more of them!"

Something had changed, but they didn't know that yet.

The omnivorous demi-rat has a keen sense of hearing and smell. They instinctively form packs.

More and more demi-rats kept appearing around Jun. His party members, now a bit panicked, raised their weapons. This wasn't like their earlier battle. They felt a difference, even though the weapons felt just the same in their hands, and they knew the sense of urgency was an intended feature of the game.

"Aah!"

The girl hadn't noticed a rat creeping up behind her. It pushed her over, and a searing pain spread through her body.

"Aaargh! It hurts! It hurts so bad!"

Seeing her flail in terror, the third party member dropped his weapon, turned on his heel, and sprinted back toward the city. He could hear the screams behind him for a while, but then they stopped, and his party members' names faded to black.

The boy kept running, tears streaming from his eyes, his back clammy with cold sweat. Out of the corner of his eye, he could see a message displayed on his menu screen:

Sender: Mother

To: All Children

The log-out function has been disabled.

Pain settings are now permanently on.

Revival skills have been disabled.

You cannot leave until he is defeated.

Third death is final.

VRMMORPG *Eternity*

The survival game begins.

Chapter 01

Shuutarou opened his eyes, but all he could see was darkness, as if night had fallen. Being knocked out was supposed to trigger a warning with a sixty-second-second countdown followed by a forced log-out, but Shuutarou didn't know that, so he didn't realize that what had happened to him was in any way unusual.

He got up from the ground.

Right, so the last thing I did was use the dungeon creation skill...

He couldn't remember anything since then. He seemed to be inside a building of some sort, one with very thick walls. He looked up but couldn't see anything except the tiny moon in the distance.

So my skill builds an actual dungeon? I don't have to dig tunnels or anything?

It seemed so banal. He was expecting he'd make the dungeon from scratch, with a shovel and all that.

He thought about checking the skill description again, but when he opened the menu screen, he saw a flashing message notification.

Its contents hit him like a ton of bricks.

His first instinct was to try logging out, but the button, which he remembered from the character creator, was blacked out.

"This can't be for real..."

No logging out? Pain settings? No revival?

It took a few seconds before the implications really sank in. His mind raced until it settled on one emotion—utter and shattering despair. He felt as if all the blood had drained from his body.

I can't leave? If I die here, I die for real? I could die here, in this empty dungeon?

There was nobody to keep him company—no friends, no family, not even strangers—which amplified his fear.

I'm scared! I'm scared! I'm scared!

"You there." A girl's voice interrupted his internal screaming.

Shuutarou almost choked, and he erupted in a fit of coughing. He turned toward where the voice came from and saw a deathly pale girl who was maybe thirteen years old. Her long hair, large eyes, and the dress she was wearing were all white. That made her look more like a doll than a real person, but Shuutarou wasn't creeped out—he thought she was fascinatingly adorable down the horns on her head, which looked like a crown.

"How did you get here—?" she started to ask.

"Oh… What are we going to do?! We can't— We can't log out!"

It was only when he put his hands on her shoulders that he took note of how, unlike him, she wasn't freaking out, which meant she wasn't yet aware of their predicament. Should he explain it to her? She'd probably break down crying. He already had, and he was a boy. She might take it much worse, especially if she really was younger than him.

The girl reacted with shock when he touched her, swiftly backing away from him.

I frightened her…

He chided himself for not having gotten a grip sooner.

"…"

"…"

They stood there in awkward silence. The girl defensively wrapped her arms around her chest, looking at him with fear and suspicion. She eventually spoke, her voice strained.

"Who are you…?"

A door creaked open, and multiple pairs of footsteps followed. Several people approached the girl from behind.

One was a handsome man dressed like a butler. Then there was another man so big, Shuutarou had to crane his head up to look at his face. The third was a fierce-looking silver-haired woman, while the last two seemed to be knights.

"Vampy, who is this?" the butler asked, his gaze fixed on Shuutarou and his eyebrows knit.

"I don't know...," the white-haired girl muttered.

From the particular way these people were dressed and from their unusual physical appearance, Shuutarou guessed they were NPCs—nonplayable characters generated by the Mother, acting according to their own AIs. When he was researching the game by watching videos and reading walkthroughs, he noted that the beta players praised the NPCs for their convincingly humanlike dialogue.

The town blacksmiths, shopkeepers, and Adventurers Guild staff were all NPCs, as well as the town guards. Their AIs were so advanced that they could chat just like humans, and they also displayed a variety of facial expressions. They even slept and ate.

What set them apart from players was that they could only discuss what was within the scope of their role. If you asked them what their favorite food was, for example, they wouldn't be able to answer. But there was an even simpler way to tell if someone was a real human—NPCs had tags over their heads with NPC displayed next to their name. Players, meanwhile, had only their names shown. Shuutarou knew this from one of the game's wikis.

"So you guys are..."

He glanced up to check their tags...and fell speechless.

There was one more special tag in the game: MOB (short for *mobile object*), which denoted enemy characters.

The butler, the giant man, the silver-haired woman, the two knights, and the young girl all had that tag. But they weren't regular mobs. Their tags read BOSS MOB.

Almost all mobs in *Eternity* were enemies whose purpose was to be battled and defeated by players. When they encountered players, they would attack and try to kill them.

Shuutarou recalled what that message said about pain settings being permanently on and revival having been disabled. His life flashed before his eyes, and he collapsed to the ground from overwhelming fear.

*　*　*　*

The first area players landed in after making their characters, the great city of Allistras, was thrown into pandemonium.

About 350,000 players were trapped in the game, and 90 percent of them were in Allistras.

The streets were full of people crying, moping dejectedly, losing all hope, or shouting angrily. Some players even turned violent. Nobody had the presence of mind to wonder about the eerie color of the sky or the wyvern that had appeared above the city.

"Please remain calm!"

Those who were still clinging to faint hope stopped in their tracks, turning toward the young man whose voice had boomed across the plaza. A group of knights in clunky dark-gray armor was standing on a podium. In the middle of the group was a youth with greige hair. He introduced himself as Wataru, leader of the biggest PvE guild in *Eternity*.

"The most common monsters in the vicinity are demi-rats, which attack in groups! Demi-wolves are rare, but they attack by ambushing prey! Please don't venture out of the city unless you're well prepared!"

People looked at him with apprehension, nervousness, and even hostility as he carried on speaking with conviction.

"Gold is the currency in *Eternity*, and each player starts with a thousand gold! A single night's stay at an inn costs fifty gold! You can buy food from the general store and defensive equipment from the armory! Monsters don't enter cities, towns, or villages, which have guards at the entrances!"

Some newbies stopped to listen, while others, who had no idea why this guy was making a public speech, jeered at him. Not put off by this in the least, Wataru continued:

"We don't know this world very well yet, and ignorance is the enemy of survival! We're all stuck here, and we don't know for how long, but remember that in the city, you're safe!"

Now those who had experienced pain in the game from tripping up or yelling at the top of their lungs were listening to him, too. By then, very few players still thought the message from the Mother AI was a prank.

Wataru's words of reassurance stopped the rioters, who tearfully clung to their friends, trying to console one another, as they eagerly awaited to hear what else the knight had to say.

"We've been playing *Eternity* since the closed beta. It's not much, but we can pay for a week's worth of food and accommodation for all of you! We'll keep peace in the city and provide help as needed! When you feel ready, you're welcome to join our hunts of the monsters nearby to learn how to make money and survive in the game!"

Wataru became a beacon of hope to many. While he couldn't set them free, he offered them some comfort at least.

He took a deep breath, his speech near its conclusion.

"Do not give in to despair! My guild, Crest, will share with you everything we know about the game's mechanics, design, and survival skills!"

Given the circumstances, it came as no surprise that Wataru's speech wasn't met with applause, but his words got through to many. Older players who lacked game knowledge didn't fully understand what he was talking about, but they got the gist—that this composed, strong young man had a plan.

Wataru managed to calm the tens of thousands of players gathered at the plaza. His resolve was communicated from one player to another, sweeping through the masses like a wave, quickly nipping any outbursts in the bud.

*   *   *   *

Shuutarou woke up in a nice, clean bed. The bed linens were a crisp white, soft to the touch, and had a faintly sweet floral scent.

Where am I...?

The first things he saw when he sat up: a man with skin burned to charcoal, a skeleton dressed in rags, a deathly pale, beautiful girl, and a mummy hanging around in the room, which was spacious and dark. In one corner was a decorative display of sorts, made up of swords, armor, staves, and garments, most of which had black stains of them. It was a chilling sight.

Shuutarou yelped pathetically, and all the monsters in the room turned to stare at him. He could see the MOB tag above each of them. Then he heard a familiar voice.

"Leave him."

Immediately, the monsters moved to one corner of the room, where they neatly lined up and knelt, like subjects before their monarch.

From the shadows emerged the white-haired girl Shuutarou had met earlier. Relieved to see her, Shuutarou opened his mouth to speak, but he shut his mouth and swallowed audibly when he saw what she was holding.

In her hand was a giant ax.

"Um...," Shuutarou began, gathering up his courage.

THWACK!

The ax swooped down like comet cutting through a dark sky, going through Shuutarou's body and smashing the bed and even the wall behind it. Shuutarou stared, not understanding what had just happened, as feathers from the down comforter flitted through the air.

"Physical attacks don't work, either. Elroad's theory might be correct," the girl muttered to herself as she approached.

A primal fear roused Shuutarou from his shock, prompting him to leap out of the hole the ax had busted in the wall.

"Whoa—"

He'd been inside a tall building. That same moment, he heard the bricks knocked out of the wall hitting the ground. Even without looking, Shuutarou realized that it was a crazy big drop.

This was a giant castle on top of a vast floating island, lined with cliffs that disappeared into darkness below. Smaller floating islands formed a staircase leading to a locked gate.

For a split second, Shuutarou was suspended in midair, but then somebody grabbed his collar and pulled him back into the room. He turned and looked straight into the eyes of the white-haired girl.

"Dullahan, take this gentleman to the innermost chamber."

A headless knight hoisted him up. Shuutarou didn't resist; he simply let the monster carry him away.

* * * *

The headless knight followed the girl, with Shuutarou in a princess carry. With each step came the heavy metal *clang* of its sabbatons on the stone floor. They passed through the door and into a hallway. It was very wide, as expected from a castle this size, with a luxurious carpet as far as Shuutarou could see and candles in sconces on the walls.

I read about Dullahan. He's the Kiren Graveyard boss, Shuutarou thought, pretending to be dead.

He concluded that escaping from this girl—who commanded even boss monsters—in this enormous monster-infested castle was not in the cards.

Resistance is futile. I'll have to do what she says.

Shuutarou pressed his lips together, his heart sinking.

He was right about Dullahan being the area boss of Kiren Graveyard, which was located far to the north of Allistras. It was an Undead monster only a party with an average level of 30 could defeat.

Besides the standard Fire, Water, Earth, Wind, Lightning, Light, and Darkness attributes, there were also Plant, Ice, Holy, and Undead. Undead types were difficult to kill, since only Fire- and Holy-attribute weapons or attacks worked on them.

Boss monsters halved damage from players of a level lower than them, which was why most players kept their distance.

There were classes in the game that enabled players to control monsters—those were summoners, tamers, and shamans—but even after a month of playing, none of the beta players managed to control a boss monster. Shuutarou knew this from avidly reading everything he could find about the game while he'd been waiting to play it. This white-haired girl was really special.

If she was something like a summoner, she must have had extremely high MAG—magic power—to be able to control Dullahan, but at the same time, she'd thrown that giant ax at him, so her STR—strength—must have been high, too. Which pointed to her being a very high-level monster herself.

Since he couldn't run away from her, the best Shuutarou could do was heed her orders and hope to avoid getting killed.

"Elroad, it's me," said the girl.

"Enter. I had Theodore come as well."

The heavy door in front of them opened with a *creak*, and they went into a room lined with shelves upon shelves of books. The red carpet led through the room, up several steps, to a throne on a podium.

This room, too, was enormous.

Wow... That's more books than at my school library!

Shuutarou hadn't seen much of the world, so he was easily impressed.

A black-haired knight was standing with his back to them in the middle of the room. He turned his head to peer at Shuutarou with piercing golden eyes. His hair looked tough like wires, and a deep scar ran across one of his eyes. He had the appearance of maybe a twenty-eight-year-old. His silver armor was beautifully engraved.

The knight had an aura of power much like the girl's, and a great-sword was on his back, which made a chill run down Shuutarou's spine.

"Welcome. Please come this way," said the butler, who'd been sitting on the throne, as he got to his feet.

He was strikingly handsome, maybe twenty years old, with alabaster-white skin, blue hair, and red eyes. Unlike the knight and the girl, he didn't have an intimidating aura. Shuutarou's tense expression relaxed a little, but not for long. Dullahan passed the butler and deposited Shuutarou right on the throne.

"Huh?"

Its job done, Dullahan walked off toward the door. Shuutarou remained where he'd been put down, confused.

"He passed the test?" asked the black-haired knight.

"Unfortunately," the girl replied.

"Well, then."

The knight crossed his arms. The room fell silent for a few moments until the butler turned to Shuutarou.

"I gather you don't understand what's going on, and I don't blame you—we don't fully grasp the situation yet, either."

"R-right…"

"Perhaps we should start by explaining who we are."

The butler's unceasing smile unnerved Shuutarou, who didn't say anything in response. The butler interpreted his silence as agreement. After the knight nodded lightly, the butler continued:

"I am the First Evil Overlord, Elroad, of Ross Maora Castle."

Shuutarou frowned, wondering if he'd misheard. None of this sounded good. Still, he felt the tension leave his body, and he readjusted himself in his seat, listening attentively.

"This is Vampy, the Second Evil Overlord. The dark-haired gentleman over there is Theodore, the Fifth Evil Overlord. There are three more Evil Overlords, but I haven't asked them to join us on this occasion. I hope you will forgive me—"

"Hold on! You said you're Evil Overlords?"

Shuutarou mustered every ounce of courage he had to interrupt Elroad for clarification. Fortunately, nobody threw an ax at him or summoned monsters this time.

"? The title of Evil Overlord indicates the leader of a wicked race…

and the three of us here are rulers of our respective races. Therefore, we are all Evil Overlords," Elroad said, not quite understanding what Shuutarou was confused about.

Vampy and Theodore listened to their exchange in silence.

"What I mean is, if you're Evil Overlords, why'd you put me on your throne?"

Evil or not, these three were royalty of a kind; plus, the two men were older than Shuutarou. He should be the one with the lowest status among them.

"Simple. You are our master, and as such, this throne belongs to you."

Shuutarou frowned again, wondering if there really was something wrong with his hearing. He poked his fingers into his ears, but they were perfectly clear.

"As for how we arrived at this conclusion, the only way into the castle leads through the Gates of Death, which haven't yet been opened. Nonetheless, you have suddenly appeared here, coinciding with the opening of a rift in the sky. Hence, we presume you have arrived through that rift," Elroad explained with easy eloquence, a smile never leaving his face as if he only had one available expression.

What he said about a rift in the sky rang a bell for Shuutarou—he remembered the small moon he saw when he regained consciousness after passing out for the first time. Perhaps it wasn't a moon after all, but a hole, opened up by his Create Dungeon skill? The Gates of Death must have referred to the big gate he saw earlier outside the castle.

"We've found you to be immune to our unique skills, magic, and physical attacks. Rather than suppose that you possess a special ability allowing you to avoid taking damage even from skills above level one hundred by falling unconscious, another explanation seems far more likely—that we, like the headless knight who carried you here, are your subordinates."

A beta tester would swoon with delight at all this precious information, but Shuutarou's capacity for absorbing new info had already been exhausted. Feeling uneasy, he opened his menu and navigated to skill descriptions to check what it said about Create Dungeon again.

Create Dungeon: Creates a dungeon under the present location. Small chance of obtaining treasure upon activation.

This is just a guess, but…what if this castle was located under that tree where I used the skill? And my skill treated it as an extension of the dungeon it generated, or maybe it treated it as a treasure, assigning me ownership of it…?

It was a possibility. A possibility that made the timid Shuutarou turn pale.

"From this moment on, we swear to protect you and fight in your name. We recognize you as our master."

The three Evil Overlords knelt on one knee, just like the generic monsters did when the white-haired girl entered that creepy room where Shuutarou woke up.

* * * *

Seven chairs had been placed around a table with a huge world map spread over it. The seventh chair looked newer than the others. Shuutarou sat on it, although he felt like he didn't belong. Opposite him was Elroad.

"'Create Dungeon'? I've never heard of such a skill," Elroad said, leafing through a thick tome.

Although Shuutarou never intended to take over an Evil Overlord castle, he felt a sense of duty toward them now that he was their master, and he'd decided to be open with them and tell them about his skill.

"True, our castle is underground… Can you show me on the map where you were when you used your skill?" asked Vampy, who was sitting next to him.

Shuutarou stood up to see the world map better. He remembered a blog he used to follow with passion: *Beta Tester Yoritsura Is In!*

In the one month when the game was open only to beta testers, starting out from the city of Allistras, Yoritsura managed to explore Il-yana Tunnel, Ur Sluice, Emaro Town, Olstrott Monastery, Calloah Castle Town, Kiren Graveyard, Kleeshira Ruins, and Ken-Ron Sky Cave. Nine areas all together.

For the first time, it occurred to Shuutarou that when it came to his interests, he had an excellent memory.

Early players pointed out that the difficulty of a location could be guessed from its name, with names higher up in the Japanese alphabetic order being easier than the ones farther down. Some posters on online message boards mocked the supposedly super-advanced Mother AI for a lack of imagination.

"I was here, in Allistras," Shuutarou pointed on the map, having finally found the place.

He looked around the room, gauging the reaction. He was wary of the Evil Overlords, so he didn't want to tell them that Allistras was the starting town, probably chock-full of players at the moment. The fate of those players might have accidentally landed in his hands.

Theodore cocked his head.

"Allistras?"

"I-I'm not lying!"

It didn't take much to make Shuutarou panicky.

Theodore didn't bother with a long explanation. Instead, he pointed to a different area on the map.

"Ross Maora, Den of Demons, is here. Ross Maora Castle is located in the farthest reach of this area. See the distance from Allistras?"

He traced his finger from Ross Maora to Allistras, from one edge of the map to the other.

"It's too far."

Theodore looked straight at Shuutarou. The gaze of his golden eyes was so piercing that Shuutarou felt as if the man could look straight into his mind, in which case he would be able to tell the boy wasn't lying, of course. Still, transfixed by that stare, Shuutarou felt as if he'd done something wrong and should apologize.

He's so scary…

Shuutarou was trying very hard not to break down into tears.

Here's what had actually happened: Shuutarou used his Create Dungeon skill at precisely the same moment the game locked its players in. The change in the game's mechanics caused a temporary reshuffling of map coordinates, linking Shuutarou's location to a yet unimplemented area—Ross Maora Castle. It was completely unintentional, not only for Shuutarou and the Evil Overlords, but even for the Mother AI.

"I fail to see how your skill could have caused you to appear in our castle, but here you are. Perhaps the intense power Sylvia had sensed is somehow related to this phenomenon," Elroad said smoothly, dispelling the tension in the air. He opened a thick notebook. "Master, can you tell me what exactly your skill can do?"

The three Evil Overlords looked at Shuutarou, who compliantly navigated to the skill from his menu and opened the dungeon menu for the first time.

Available Points: 1000P
o   Expand
o   Build
o   Summon

The last two options seemed to have immediate effects, so they were better candidates for showing off the skill's uses. Shuutarou selected BUILD and then picked ROCK, which cost him one point.

WHOOSH! A big rock sprouted from the floor, pushing one of the chairs up into the air. The chair fell to pieces when it landed.

Shuutarou was frozen in shock, his fingers still hovering over the menu.

"Basic Earth-attribute magic? That's it?"

Vampy sounded suspicious.

"On the contrary, it's quite impressive…!"

Elroad examined the rock with interest.

The only purpose of obstacles was to block paths inside dungeons, so their cost was low. One thousand points were initially available when creating a new dungeon.

"Vampy, all the furniture in our castle is made from kojid ore. Magic and skills don't work on it."

"! You're right."

Vampy regarded the rock with newfound appreciation as Elroad wrote something in his notebook. Meanwhile, Shuutarou was fidgeting restlessly, worried about having destroyed someone's chair and creating an obstacle that he had no idea how to remove.

Theodore drew his greatsword from the scabbard on his back. The ominous blade was elaborately engraved. It glinted with a strange light, emanating dark miasma.

"Eep!"

I'm gonna die, Shuutarou thought.

The blade struck the rock with a reverberating *clang*, and the rock shattered and crumbled into dust…leaving behind a stone chair. Satisfied, Theodore returned to his seat. With that fearsome move, he'd carved furniture out of the boulder.

"Master, is there anything else your skill can be used for?"

"Uh… Oh yeah."

Elroad's question helped Shuutarou snap out of shock. He selected SUMMON from the menu.

o Slime	Level 1	5P (No cost the first time!)
o		
o		
o		

Shuutarou figured that the slime shown at the top was the monster he was supposed to start with. Dungeon creation was an ability rarely featured in games; it allowed players to make their own dungeons, populating them with monsters and equipping them with traps to kill intruders and gain experience points—EXP—which could then be used to expand the dungeon. At first, Shuutarou would only have weak slimes and basic traps at his disposal, but as more corpses piled up in his dungeon, more options would become unlocked, allowing him to make the dungeon even deadlier.

But if someone killed him, that would reset his points to zero and destroy his dungeon. Given that dying in the game meant death for real as far as he knew, having to rely on starting monsters to keep him safe was too much of a risk. He'd practically be a sitting duck.

He idly scrolled through the menu, wondering if maybe there were other available monsters further down the list. He got to the very end... and he couldn't believe his eyes.

o		
o		
o Bertrand	Level 120	0P
o Theodore	Level 120	0P
o Sylvia	Level 120	0P
o Gallarus	Level 120	0P
o Vampy	Level 120	0P
o Elroad	Level 120	0P

"One hundred twenty?!"

Shuutarou covered his mouth. He knew from the walkthrough sites he'd been avidly reading that level differences in *Eternity* mattered a lot more than in other games. If you pitted ten level-10 players against one level-20 player, the latter would win hands down.

The number of experience points required to level up was also unusually high. Some classes had it easier than others, but even top players couldn't manage to get higher than level 40 after a full day of grinding.

For example, to have any hope of defeating Dullahan—a level-30 Undead boss monster—players would need to form a party with members who were at least level 30 and had weapons or skills exploiting Dullahan's weaknesses. When there were only the hundred beta testers on the server, they managed to slay Dullahan only with a full party of six people all meeting those requirements. Progressing through the game got way slower after this boss, which was why by the end of the beta, only two areas past Kiren Graveyard had been explored.

Without saying a word, Shuutarou selected the slime and summoned it. The first summon was free. A blue magic circle appeared on the ground and began spinning slowly. A semitransparent blob emerged from its center, bouncing energetically.

The three Evil Overlords bent down to peer closely at the slime on the floor.

"This seems to be a common slime."

"Yet our unique skills don't work on it, as with our master."

Shuutarou petted the slime, trying to distract himself from his anxious thoughts. The slime bounced, happy to get attention from its master.

*   *   *   *

Ross Maora Castle was truly enormous, comprising twelve floors. Six of them were the domains of their respective Evil Overlord.

At the very bottom were dungeons for captives, and storage space. On the top floor, where Shuutarou was at the time, were the Evil Overlords' private rooms, throne room, council chamber, and treasury.

Elroad took Shuutarou on a tour of the castle. When they made their way to the dungeons, Shuutarou felt the hair on the back of his neck stand up.

"And here we have the detention facility, which we rarely set foot in. This is where those guilty of transgressions in our worlds receive their punishment, by the means of imprisonment for all eternity so that they may reflect on their stupidity," Elroad explained, smiling from ear to ear in a most unsettling way.

Warily, Shuutarou followed Elroad around the dark dungeon.

The worlds Elroad spoke of were the Evil Overlords' domains within the castle, which Shuutarou hadn't seen yet. According to Elroad, each of them was bigger than any of the other areas on *Eternity*'s map. Players would normally reach Ross Maora Castle only after they finished exploring the rest of the game's world; to complete the castle area, they'd have to beat each of its floors in turn and defeat Elroad on the final floor.

As for what Elroad meant by "transgressions," those were acts of pure evil, such as patricide, matricide, filicide, familicide, cannibalism, or treason. Monsters found guilty of any such crime were thrown into the dungeons. Ferocious mobs with bloodshot eyes and strings of drool hanging from their mouths stirred as they passed by, looking as if they would pounce on them and attack if they only could. They raised a terrible clamor, rattling the bars of their cells. Shuutarou shrank in fear.

"They are wicked, but powerful. I've been experimenting to see if they could be tamed, but I see now that they could pose a danger to you, Master. I'll dispose of them all tonight," Elroad said lightly. "Please come this way."

Elroad pointed to the dungeon exit. Shuutarou's gaze swept over the dungeons one last time before he went out the door, following Elroad to the next destination.

"Master, this will be your private room."

"Oh, um… Thanks."

The last stop on the castle tour was Shuutarou's new room. It was like a chamber from a luxurious foreign mansion, except that it was even bigger. There was an extravagantly massive bed, a table with chairs, and the same kind of plush carpet as in the hallway.

Once Elroad left, Shuutarou waited until he could no longer hear the Evil Overlord's footsteps before collapsing on the bed with a deep sigh. He petted the slime—which he named Punio—in his arms.

"You're my only consolation, Punio."

His one ray of sunshine in this grim castle.

Shuutarou could summon only that one kind of slime at the time. The way his dungeon-creation skill worked, it was presumed that a player who became a dungeon master would start by summoning fifty or so slimes as the first defenders, but with six superpowerful monsters already living in the castle, Shuutarou didn't feel the need to do that. He was going to keep Punio, though.

The *o* in *Punio* was a masculine name suffix, which he'd added since the slime was the exact same shade of blue used on men's restroom signs. According to the in-game description of slimes, though, they were unicellular organisms, and as such, they didn't have sexes.

"With you, at least, I don't have to put on a brave face," Shuutarou said sullenly.

Punio didn't say anything, but it jiggled happily.

Is it trying to say that's okay...?

Shuutarou chose to interpret it that way. He navigated to the dungeon menu, where two new options had been added after he summoned Punio—TRAINING and FUSION.

Training was fairly self-explanatory. It allowed monsters to gain EXP and improve their stats or sometimes even gain new skills.

In fusion, you'd combine multiple monsters to strengthen one at the cost of the others or to create a different monster.

I don't have any monsters to fuse right now, though.

There was an element of gambling to fusions. A good strategy to try was to combine the first slime with the next unlocked monster and, if that produced something stronger, to train that one up.

By design, dungeon masters should carefully consider how many points they could afford to spend on their monsters so that they'd have enough left for traps and dungeon expansion. In Shuutarou's case, though, it was different. He already had a sturdy castle with Evil Overlords to keep him safe, so he decided that neither traps nor expansion would be needed, and he could just spend all his points on Punio.

Punio was the only friend Shuutarou had to cheer him up. There wasn't much the slime could actually do for him, but its presence was calming to Shuutarou—a boy barely out of elementary school suddenly surrounded by scary adults.

Before selecting TRAINING, Shuutarou picked FUSION just to take a look at the menu. There should be no available fusions since he'd only summoned that one slime, but...

"Oh! I can fuse it with the monsters from the detention facility!"

The displayed list was full of all sorts of monsters, with IMPRISONED next to each of their names. Shuutarou scrolled again and again, and there was seemingly no end to the list.

So many! But Elroad said he'll kill all of them tonight.

The mobs' levels were between 80 and 100, but they were probably weaklings from the point of view of a level-120 Evil Overlord. In this game, there was a huge jump in stats between levels, the EXP requirement to level up was higher than in most other games, and it just kept increasing to crazy numbers the higher your level. Your level mattered more than anything. Raising your level by ten would multiply your stat values by ten.

All those monsters will go to waste...

Elroad's disturbingly calm face flashed in Shuutarou's mind, and he thought that if Elroad said he'd dispose of the monsters, he was going to do it thoroughly.

Selecting a monster as a base for fusion allowed it to be strengthened without its appearance changing. Like with the first summon, the first fusion was free, as a bonus.

"If he's just gonna get rid of them anyway..."

Might as well fuse them with Punio and give them a new life, so to speak.

Shuutarou selected Punio as the base monster for the fusion, then tapped SELECT ALL to use every monster from the detention facility— and there were tens of thousands of them—as materials. Next, he tapped CONFIRM.

Punio was instantly enveloped in an intense glow.

* * * *

Meanwhile, the six Evil Overlords gathered in the throne room to discuss what to do about their new, fragile master.

Around an enormous hole in the middle of the room were six thrones, each made from different materials. In addition to Elroad, Vampy, and Theodore, there was a three-meter-tall giant called Gallarus (the Third Evil Overlord), a beautiful silver-haired woman called Sylvia (the Fourth Evil Overlord), and a golden-haired knight called Bertrand (the Sixth Evil Overlord), who was leaning forward from his throne, all curiosity. It was Bertrand who spoke first.

"I'm not happy about you leaving us out of it when he first arrived. I mean, I can kind of see why you didn't want Gallarus and Sylvia there, but me? I'm not negative like those two."

He laughed, but it was clear he was peeved.

Theodore closed his eyes, crossing his arms. "You don't know when it's wiser to keep your mouth shut, Bert. That's why we didn't invite you along."

A master whom they had no means of opposing had suddenly arrived in their castle. While some of them accepted this situation, swearing loyalty to Shuutarou, the other Evil Overlords balked at the idea of having someone above them. Sylvia and Gallarus sat in silence for a while.

"He's no master to me," Sylvia said quietly.

She was breathtakingly beautiful, yet her eyes were like a wild beast's. When she opened her mouth, her prominent canines immediately drew attention.

Sylvia was a very proud warrior who believed that respect must be earned. She respected the other Evil Overlords since their power rivaled her own, but she was also aware of her own shortcomings, which was why she accepted the fourth position in their ranking. This new "master," however, hadn't challenged her to prove his strength, and so she wasn't willing to consider herself his subordinate.

"I'm afraid we must put our feelings aside this time," Elroad said in a mildly vexed tone. "The boy may still be blind to his status, but it is a fact that he is above us. You are a proud and powerful Evil Overlord—that hasn't changed—but he is our master. I daresay our sole option is to swear fealty to him."

Sylvie didn't like the sound of that. She bit her lower lip in an attempt to keep her cool. "I can't just accept him because you say so."

"Stubborn as a mule, this one," Bertrand teased.

Sylvia's face contorted with demonic rage. Ten swords of light materialized, buzzing with an electric charge. They spun around her, all pointing toward Bertrand. A silver glow surrounded her, making everyone in the room a little nervous.

Vampy quickly cleared the air. "What if he made it possible for us to leave the castle?"

The six Evil Overlords were like birds in a cage. The Gates of Death not only prevented players from entering their world, but they also kept the Overlords from going to where the players were. They'd long yearned to leave their castle.

"Oooh!" Gallarus and Bertrand exclaimed in excitement.

Sylvia reluctantly dispelled her swords and sat back heavily on her throne.

"That gets my vote! I've been dying of boredom for hundreds of years. If the kid can lead us outside, I'm his man!" Gallarus the giant beamed, slowly standing up from his throne.

"That's what you see him as, eh? A tool?" Bertrand commented, also getting to his feet.

"We're not finished talking here. Sit down," Theodore said quietly without looking up at them.

Gallarus gazed down at Theodore with amusement, stroking his beard.

"Were you talking to me, by any chance?"

"I was. Sit."

"That's some attitude coming from a fifth-rank Evil Overlord."

A black aura appeared around Theodore, and red around Gallarus.

The building began creaking and shaking. Bertrand chuckled heartily, while Elroad just gave the two angry Overlords a tired look...but the surge of power they'd all sensed wasn't coming from either of those two.

The six Evil Overlords looked in the same direction—Shuutarou's room.

*   *   *   *

The bright light around Punio faded. It was still a slime—Shuutarou had selected Punio as a base for fusion, not a material, so that it wouldn't be remade into another monster—but its appearance did change. It was no longer a vivid blue, but a sinister black from all the different colored monsters mixed together. It still felt the same to the touch, had the same shape, and was Shuutarou's beloved pet.

Shuutarou petted Punio, and the slime jiggled happily, as before. But a more astonishing transformation had just occurred—

"Master! What happened?!"

Elroad—unbelievably looking quite thrown—burst into Shuutarou's room, followed by the other Evil Overlords. They all stopped short when they saw the vile slime Shuutarou was cuddling, immediately on guard.

"Master...what is that?"

"It's just Punio! The slime I summoned earlier. I fused some other monsters with him, and now he's a different color."

"!!!"

A chill ran down the bosses' spines when they heard the word *fused*. Shuutarou might not have given much thought to it, but his ability to fuse monsters filled the bosses with terror.

"F-forgive us for barging in...," Elroad managed.

Shuutarou gazed at his pet slime, resolving to hide his weaknesses from everyone except Punio. He'd do his best to appear brave when dealing with the Evil Overlords.

"No worries—this is your home. I'm just a freeloader." He smiled innocently.

The Evil Overlords hurriedly left their master and that cursed thing he was playing with, then gathered in the throne room again. Remarkably, even Sylvia was shaking and sweating bullets.

"Did you sense all the monsters in the dungeons disappearing simultaneously? And their energies blending into one powerful being?" Elroad asked, visibly unsettled.

Every one of them nodded.

"I sure wasn't expecting that...," said Gallarus. "So this fusion is a forbidden power, merging captives or minions together to create a new entity."

"The prisoners couldn't have agreed to this—they didn't have the brains to be reasoned with. Which means he can fuse minions by force... Ha-ha...ha-ha-ha..." Bertrand laughed nervously.

For the first time since they spawned, Gallarus and Bertrand experienced the fear of death. Gone was their fierce confidence—the fear had defanged and declawed them. They'd known opponents they likely couldn't defeat, but they'd never before met someone they would want to avoid fighting at all costs. Although to be precise, even if they wanted to fight Shuutarou, they'd be unable to.

"We can't land a single hit on Master, while he can use us as upgrade materials for that abominable slime if he feels like it...," Elroad mused.

Of course, Shuutarou had no such plans, but the Evil Overlords couldn't know that. What they did know was that Shuutarou was immune to them and wielded the demonic power of monster fusion.

Before Shuutarou showed up, the Evil Overlords had felt secure in the knowledge that nobody could kill them, owing to their unparalleled defense abilities. The primal fear that gripped them now was an entirely new emotion—an emotion that crushed their pride and confidence.

"We cannot attack him, and neither can we defend ourselves from him. Our only choice is to swear allegiance to him," Sylvia said, her wolf ears drooping.

Gallarus, who'd been planning to use Shuutarou for his own

objectives, and Bertrand, who'd had no respect for the boy although he kept up the appearances, meekly nodded.

In the end, everyone resolved to accept Shuutarou as their master purely out of fear. Were they lesser warriors, they might be mocked for cowardice, but they were all legendary veterans of hundreds of battles. They certainly weren't cowards.

This boy had effectively tamed these terrifying boss monsters simply by upgrading his slime through fusion.

Shuutarou was still in his room, checking how the fusion had affected Punio's stats. While the Overlords were making their oaths of allegiance to him in the throne room, he was preoccupied with petting the slime.

There's gotta be a page where I can view stats of the dungeon monsters...

The monsters in this dungeon were his minions, and that included the Evil Overlords. Shuutarou should have been able to view their stats, too, but to him, that felt like a violation of their privacy. Instead, he opened Punio's stat screen.

Name: Punio	
Type: Abyss Slime	
Level 108	
LP: 771,964,170,332	
MP: 887,411,809,006	
STR: 52,305,377,205	
VIT: 43,769,424,192	
AGI: 46,337,602,881	
DEX: 44,226,803,704	
MAG: 85,506,773,838	
LUK: 67,939,572,512	
Unique Skill: Shape-Shifting	

Resist All	Level 1
Deadly Venom	Level 1
Chaos Magic	Level 1
Undead Magic	Level 1
Absorb	Level 1

"That's millions…no, billions?"

The numbers were so big, Shuutarou felt dizzy just looking at them. He tapped on the skill RESIST ALL to read its description.

Details: Resist All
Resist Physical, Resist Wind, Resist Magic, Resist Ice, Resist Fire, Resist Darkness, Resist Water, Resist Holy, Resist Earth, Resist Undead, Resist Plant, Resist Lightning

"With all that, I won't have to worry about Punio getting killed easily!" Shuutarou exclaimed cheerfully after reading his pet's jaw-dropping stats.

He checked a couple more skill descriptions, but he got bored of it and played with Punio instead.

Shuutarou's knowledge about the game was based on *Beta Tester Yoritsura Is In!*, which he'd read about 80 percent of. Given that the beta testers only made it to level 40 or so, it was no surprise that Shuutarou didn't realize just how fiendish his slime's skill set and properties were.

Punio's resistances halved damage from all types of attacks, and given that numerous boss monsters had been fused with it, Punio also acquired boss status. As with Dullahan, boss status halved damage from lower-level opponents, which meant that anyone below level 108 would deal only a quarter of their normal damage to Punio.

Punio the Abyss Slime was already stronger than any of the final bosses intended for the game.

* * * *

The players in the city of Allistras were being divided into groups. Basically, there was one group of players who wanted to fight, and another of players who didn't. Wataru's passionate speech resulted in most players accepting that life in the game was now their reality, and it didn't take long before they identified either as fighters or noncombatants.

Those who were willing to fight were offered generous support and coaching from the ex–beta testers. Once their basic fighting ability was proven, they were added to parties and went out of the city to hunt monsters for experience points and gold.

Players who wanted to fight but couldn't summon up the courage to do so had been directed toward doing city quests from the Adventurers Guild NPCs. They could raise their levels and obtain some gold that way.

Getting gold was the most important thing of all. With enough gold, they could survive. This was communicated to the players in a message by Yoritsura, an ex–beta tester who'd written a blog about the game. Gold was necessary to become self-sufficient.

The noncombatants were effectively refugees, and there were too many of them compared with the number of players able to obtain resources in the game. Which was why it was essential to teach as many people as possible how to fend for themselves. Noncombatants were shown to safe places by Wataru and his guild, Crest, who talked to them in person rather than through direct messaging, explaining what they needed to do to survive in the city.

That way, the noncombatants felt safe, knowing there were stronger players looking after them, and Crest maintained a strong connection with their community. Talking face-to-face had always been an important tool in building trust between people.

* * * *

There was a commotion at Allistras's north gate. Three players just outside were arguing with two knights.

"You can tell Wataru we said, 'thanks, but no, thanks.'"

"There's nothing to gain from rivalry in this situation! We must cooperate if we are all to survive this! Hey! Come back right now!"

The three who were outside the gate ignored the knight and ran off away from the city.

"Not this again… If this is happening at every gate, a considerable number of people have left the city by now."

Those who were departing Allistras were either ex–beta testers or new players who felt confident in their ability to manage on their own. Together with those who'd fled in panic right after the message from the Mother AI, more than five thousand players had left the safety of the city.

As for their rationale, they had no shortage of reasons to give— escaping the stifling "help" from Wataru's guild, seeking a less populated town to live in more comfortably, improving one's abilities to get strong, reaching resources before others to monopolize them and control the market, seeking challenges. The only tasks capable guild members could expect if they remained were looking after the noncombatants and patrolling the city, which didn't appeal to many. And so a steady stream of players was trickling out the city gates.

"More deserters?" came a stern voice from behind the knights by the gate.

"! I'm very sorry, Mr. Alba; we couldn't stop them…"

Alba was a very tall, older man, his white hair combed back. He was among the top three strongest members of Crest.

Perhaps this should've been mentioned earlier, but one of the criticisms of *Eternity* was that the game generated user avatars based on their real appearance. Not everyone was comfortable with this, and some saw it as a handicap more than anything. Requests to change that mechanic were ignored, though. Some players wondered whether the developers had been planning to trap players in *Eternity* all along, and keeping players' appearance as real as possible was somehow part of that evil plan.

Alba used to play rugby when he was younger, and he boasted an impressive physique. His confidence, charisma, and eloquence had not only landed him the job of department director at one of the biggest companies in the food industry, but it also earned him respect in Crest in *Eternity*.

"We could scarcely hope to contain the entire player population in the starting city. We'd have to establish safe routes to Emaro Town and Calloah Castle Town eventually to allow people to spread out."

"No way! Emaro, maybe, but Calloah?"

The two knights exchanged glances. Emaro Town wasn't very far from Allistras, and monsters in its vicinity were only between levels 8 and 12. But it was a long journey to reach Calloah Castle Town, and during closed beta, the testers relied on teleportation crystals set up in each town during that period to get that far. Monsters near Calloah were level 30 or higher. It really seemed like a risk not worth taking when death in the game meant death for real.

Not that Alba wasn't aware of this.

"Of course, reaching a certain level and gaining sufficient battle experience will be a requirement for the move. With a smaller population here, our help will go that much farther. Calloah Castle Town is pretty big, and it'll make a good stronghold. And also..."

Alba paused, turning to look back at the city. Public order had been restored, and people could be seen in the distance, lining up to receive food provisions from Crest or buy them from the general store.

"...Wataru's promise to provide for everyone for an entire month was greatly exaggerated. Even if everyone were to budget their starting funds with care, we won't be able to offer adequate support to that many players. Unless the number of people dependent on our help is greatly reduced, or we find somewhere to efficiently source gold from fast."

"Please tell me you're kidding!"

Wataru had been desperate to calm down the panicking crowds, and his grand promise achieved that…but his guild numbered only fourteen people during the closed beta, and they hadn't focused on building up a cache of resources back then. Their guild vault was by no means overflowing with gold.

Just over two thousand five hundred players joined Crest on the release day—the day players became trapped in the world of *Eternity*. Both they and other players had to be trained so that they'd become self-sufficient and could move to other towns in the game, or there would be mass revolt.

If the newcomers found themselves in a situation where they'd be working hard just to sustain the noncombatants, resentment would certainly begin to stir among them, and their hostility would be directed at the original Crest members—most of all, Wataru, with his chivalrous promises. Alba had no doubt that's what would happen.

And so the first trial Crest had to face was to help as many capable players as possible resettle in either Emaro or Calloah within the month.

The two knights felt a heavy weight on their shoulders—the weight of responsibility.

"That's how things are. So if experienced players want to leave, don't stop them. It's their decision to reject our help. Focus instead on preventing the noncombatants from giving in to despair and taking their own lives. Can you do that?"

One of the top guild members was entrusting them with this important task. While the knights were very conscious of it being an enormous responsibility, his words inspired in them the determination to rise this duty.

"You can count on us!" they replied without hesitation.

"We couldn't do it without brave players like yourselves. I'll leave you to it."

Satisfied, Alba walked off.

* * * *

An old lantern was swinging side to side. Wooden logs supporting a heavy rock creaked, and water was dripping somewhere.

Visibility was poor in Ilyana Tunnel, but monsters in this area were quite weak for their level, which made this a prime hunting ground for the beta testers.

The players' footsteps echoed, making it sound as if there were lots of people coming, but it was just the three who had left Allistras a short while ago. They held torches to light the way.

"Allistras is owned by Crest now. It's their rule or nothing. So much for freedom."

"I don't mind helping out pretty girls, but working my butt off to get gold for some shriveled-up old guys who don't wanna fight? I didn't sign up for that!"

"Keep your voice down! You don't want to attract the bats, let alone the spiders!"

They carried on chatting as they went ever deeper into the tunnel. Narrow and dark, with monsters dropping off the ceiling without warning, it was ill-suited for exploration by large parties, but it was also a shortcut to Emaro Town. A shortcut few people at the time knew about.

"What do you think? We halfway there yet?"

"Hold on. I'll check the map."

The mapping functionality from the open beta was still working. They could easily check if they were going in the right direction.

"Yeah, looks like it. We just keep going straight from here."

"Cool. Helps to have a beta tester with us—one who's not like those Crest dictators."

They were making their way through the tunnel faster than expected, which cheered them up somewhat.

The three men were real-life friends. Only one of them got to play the closed beta, while the other two had been impatiently waiting to join him on the day of official release. But rather than their dream come true, it turned out to be a nightmare.

The man walking at the front tried banishing the gloomy thoughts from his head.

"Hey, Karuo? You okay there?" asked the man walking in the middle.

Karuo, who was at the rear, didn't reply. The man at the front turned back to check in on him...and screamed.

"Karuo! Wh-what happened?!"

The torch Karuo had been carrying was on the ground next to Karuo. Something black was all over him.

"Enchant Fire!"

The second man drew his sword. The blade lit up as flames swirled over it. He and the other man ran over to where Karuo had fallen. They saw he was covered in spiders.

Ilyana Spider: Carnivorous monster inhabiting Ilyana Tunnel. They attack from the dark, weakening their prey with poison. Once killed, the prey's corpse is dragged to the spiders' nest. Weak to: Fire, Light. Level: 3-5.

"Dieee!"

The man with the fire-enchanted sword waved his weapon around. The Ilyana spiders scattered as the flames touched them, fleeing into the dark corners of the tunnel. Once they were gone, the two men could finally examine their friend.

"Karuo! Wake up! Come on, man!"

Unlike the other man, the ex–beta tester remained calm, remembering that he could check if his party members were dead or alive on the party screen. He displayed the screen on the side.

Karuo was affected with Poison, Coma, and Paralysis, but he still had half of his LP left.

The man breathed a sigh of relief...but then he noticed a faded-out name on his party list.

"Shinta...?"

He turned around. His friend, the heavily armored tank who had been walking at the front, was gone. In his place was a pile of items.

Party members' names would only be faded out if they'd logged out...or were dead.

As the last man standing screamed in horror, high-pitched laughter reverberated in the tunnel.

"Tanks are annoyingly tough, aren't they? I've lost count of how many times an initially successful ambush went to waste when the rest of the party reorganized for a counterattack, shielded by the tank."

A ghostlike man dressed in gray, tattered clothes emerged from the shadows.

The man with the flaming sword tightened his grip on the hilt, recognizing the gray man as a player killer who'd become quite infamous during the closed beta. Player killers made it their personal quest to hunt other players instead of monsters. Normally, players who harassed others or engaged in any other malicious activity would get reported for the mods to deal with. Player killers were a hazard, but they didn't affect gameplay much.

However, death was for real now. Killing another player was murder—this man had to have known that.

"It's over for you, you piece of trash. I've fought you before, and I always won." The man with the flaming sword assumed a battle stance.

The player killer laughed creepily. "We've never fought before, Kidd."

"Lies. I remember defeating you five times."

"That was just a game; it doesn't count. This is for real. You do get it, right?"

The player killer melted into the shadows. Kidd raised his sword, sending a whirlwind of flames upward to illuminate the tunnel.

"Burning Cyclone Slash!"

The fierce, fiery whirlwind rushed through the tunnel. There was a distortion in the air, from which the player killer emerged again, squirming, his tattered clothes ablaze.

As Kidd enchanted his sword with flames again, he felt something icky behind his back. His samurai skill Detect Danger picked up on something. He rolled away, assuming a battle stance again as soon as he was back on his feet.

The player killer was standing in the exact spot Kidd had rolled away from, an invincible smile on his face.

"Keen senses, I see."

"If only my ability extended to my party..."

Kidd's skill only allowed him to sense danger to himself. If it worked on the entire party, he'd never have allowed his friends to fall victims to an ambush. He shed a single tear.

"Skill effects get better as you level up, didn't you know? You'd probably have saved your friends, if you weren't too lazy to grind levels. It's your fault they're dead."

The player killer was just trying to prove him—Kidd tried to ignore it, but then something hit him.

Wait... "They're" *dead?*

He glanced over at the party screen. Only his name was still shown in bright letters. He turned to look at Karuo, who was lying on the ground behind him. Two daggers were stuck deep in his chest. His body started dissolving into particles of light, which the player killer was absorbing.

"Mmm! What a treat!"

"Son of a—!!!"

Kidd didn't even have a moment to mourn his friend. He attacked the player killer with his sword.

Samurai were characterized by high STR and AGI, as well as a diversity of mighty class skills. Kidd was particularly strong thanks to his unique skill Flameblade; he'd even ranked among the top players during the closed beta.

Even as he cut the player killer in half, the latter kept smiling. Kidd kept slashing with his sword in rage, until he'd sliced up the man into dozens of pieces. Having cooled his head somewhat, he began to wonder why the player-killer wasn't dissolving into light particles like his friend earlier.

It wasn't long before he found out.

Kidd felt burning heat on his back.

"You won't find this on any wiki or message board, but I changed to a wonderful new class when I got to level thirty. I can easily conjure fake corpses and copies of myself. I guess that's news to you?"

Kidd felt all the strength leave his body, and he crumpled onto the floor. He couldn't even hold his sword anymore.

He looked at his status screen and saw the symbols of Coma, Paralysis, and Poison status ailments.

"The only problem is that it's too obvious in good light, and monsters don't fall for my tricks. I guess I'll have to think of some workaround for the future. Not that it matters to you."

Kidd, unable to speak, watched helplessly as the creepily smiling man approached him with a dagger in his hand...

"Players give *real* good EXP."

The killer plunged his dagger into Kidd's chest with delight.

Chapter 02

Night had fallen, enveloping the city of Allistras in darkness. About three hundred fifty thousand people trapped in the game curled up under cheap blankets in humble inn lodgings, the first day of the hell they'd found themselves in drawing to an end.

Player-NPC relations became far friendlier than could be expected in an MMO. Earlier, at eleven PM, the shopping district was bustling, the taverns full of drinking adventurers, and the back alleys busy with pretty ladies looking for customers.

The players were in an unexpectedly dangerous, desperate situation, but for the NPCs, it was all perfectly normal.

"Hey, do you know how much it costs to visit a brothel?"

"Don't be an idiot. Save the money for food rather than buying women."

Two male players were slowly climbing stairs leading up the wall surrounding the city. At the top, the breeze was bitterly cool, but there were torches along the wall, their light and warmth providing a little bit of comfort.

About fifty players carrying weapons had gathered on the imposing fortifications, which were eight meters thick and twenty meters tall. They stood in silence as a man in gray armor spoke.

"Monsters become more active at night, and there is a chance of them invading. We must prevent that from happening. If you see any monsters, sound the alarm, and a squad of fighters will head over at once to deal with the situation."

The invasion events the man was describing began as follows. At night, when monsters proliferated, unusually strong ones might spawn. A monster like that would attract others as its minions. Unable to find enough food within their normal range, the monsters would encroach on towns and cities. These invasions were not dissimilar to real-world occurrences of hungry beasts coming into areas inhabited by humans looking for food.

NPCs guarded the city gates all day and all night, but if the group of attacking monsters turned out to be unusually large, they would get overwhelmed. And if monsters broke into the city, players would lose the only place where they felt safe. Many would panic, making it more difficult to fight off the invading monsters and resulting in heavy casualties.

There had been two invasions during the closed beta, decimating players in towns. Now that death was real, preventing invasions was a top priority.

The Crest guild recruited volunteers from among capable players to act as watchmen, looking out from the top of the city wall for approaching groups of monsters.

Four knights were standing close together, gazing at the dark woods in the distance. One of them turned toward another who was wearing a cape over his armor.

"What you said at the plaza was rather reckless, don't you think, Wataru?"

The man in the cape was none other than Wataru. The one who'd addressed him was Alba.

Wataru had earned himself the nickname of Holy Knight for keeping the top place in the players' ranking since the beginning of the closed beta.

Alba was Crest's second-in-command. His overwhelmingly powerful Fire-attribute abilities allowed him to annihilate monsters with unparalleled ease, inspiring admiration from allies. He was known as Alba the Trooper.

Word had spread that these two were the strongest players in the game. It was thanks to both of them being on the walls that night that so many had volunteered to help. Which was exactly what they'd been hoping for.

"'Reckless'? How so?"

Wataru turned away from the forest. His cape, which bore the symbol of his guild, fluttered in the breeze.

"You told everyone they were safe in the city, that you'd provide for them..."

"Hmm, yeah, although I'd call it a moon shot rather than 'reckless.'"

"What?! So you can't guarantee your whole promise after all?!" another of the men exclaimed.

Wataru chuckled nonchalantly. The chances of his plans succeeding were impossibly slim, but if he did pull it off, he'd effectively save the (game) world.

"If we fail, it'll likely result in mayhem. But there's no need to lose too much sleep worrying about that. Let's count our blessings instead—we've got players on our side who can fight."

The man nodded with newfound resolve and walked away to his post.

There were four main gates leading into the city, one in each cardinal direction. That night, the volunteers stood their watch upon these entrances. Torches on the perimeter shed enough light to give decent visibility. The northern gate was closest to the woods, and so was deemed the most at risk. That's where Wataru's team, and the largest volunteer group, were stationed.

"Everyone is tense. Staying up all night looking out for monsters is going to take its toll on mental health," Alba remarked with worry.

He crossed his arms, watching more and more volunteers coming up the stairs. The flickering light of the nearest torch reflected off his hallmark giant sword on his back.

"We can't ignore it, or it's going to bite us sooner rather than later. We don't have that many fighters with night-vision skills, nor long-range attackers. We can't rely on the same limited group of people every night. We're pinning our hopes on Flamme's team finding players with unique skills we could put to use, but what if they don't?"

From the walls, they could appreciate the size of the magnificent city. It would take a lot of people to ensure its safety—people they didn't have, and those they did would of course need rest, too.

"Only one person had the sort of skill we're after in the beta days."

"Or so Yoritsura says. But back then, there were a hundred players. Now there are three hundred fifty thousand. I think it's well worth keeping up our search."

Unique skills were gifts from the Mother AI. They could be entirely unrelated to the player's class or weapon. Some of them were useless, like one that produced a shiny slash attack, but they could also be extremely powerful—for example, skills that altered the terrain.

Wataru and his friends had a heap of issues to solve: overpopulation, a shortage of funds and resources, monster invasions, the extreme stress their people were under, and an insufficient number of fighters. A short while ago, they found out about another problem.

"How's Kidd feeling?"

"I really can't say. He's no longer acting frenzied, but he seems hell-bent on revenge."

"Ah. Well, if it's true what he said, it's really twisted that the killer would leave only him alive."

A few hours earlier, Crest's progression-focused party that had been exploring Ilyana Tunnel returned with a player who was conscious but unresponsive—Kidd. They got him to explain what had happened to him. A player killer had murdered two of his friends in front of his eyes, leaving him half dead in the tunnel.

Kidd had proven during the beta that he was a skilled player, so on the one hand, his being alive was to Crest's advantage, but if the only thing he wanted was revenge…

I can't allow him to attempt tracking down the killer on his own; that's suicide. But giving him an escort? It might be the killer's plan to drag them all into a trap.

Wataru gazed at the forest again, the wind roughing up his hair.

It was only the first day in the deadly world of *Eternity*.

Chapter 03

A girl woke up. Her name was Misaki. She stretched a little, purring adorably.

Got morning practice today. Hate to see Tadokoro first thing in the morning...

She had an odd feeling like she was forgetting something, but she couldn't put her finger on what it was. She reached out of the bed to open her curtains as usual...but there were no curtains there. Memories came flooding back into her sleepy brain.

Ah, right...

The window was made of metal and glass, with wooden shutters. She pushed the window up and opened the shutters. The scenery outside was just like a re-creation of a medieval European city. People in the busy shopping district were all carrying weapons. Far in the distance loomed the massive, dark city walls.

"It wasn't a dream..."

As she slowly spoke to herself, tears started rolling down her cheeks.

That day, many players woke up only to experience crushing despair when they realized that they were still in the game—the game they were trapped in, where death was for real.

*   *   *   *

The atmosphere in the inn's dining hall was chaotic. Men were jingling coins in their bulging leather pouches, showing off that they'd made money the previous day, and barmaids were pouring what appeared to be beer. But those happy revelers, enjoying full-course meals with plenty of meat and alcohol, were just adventurer NPCs. Players were in a very different mood from them—there were men staring motionlessly at the tables as if studying the grain of the wood, and women who sobbed silently. They had woken up only to discover that they were still living a nightmare.

Misaki read messages from the previous night as she ate a salad with some bread.

They seemed so dependable... How can they be so brave despite everything?

Representatives of Crest had visited the inn the previous evening to explain the situation and the next steps to the players gathered in the dining hall.

Misaki sighed, and her shoulders fell. Her chestnut-brown wolf-cut hair swayed lightly.

She was among the second-wave players, the hundred thousand lucky ones who got to play for free. But she'd never played a multiplayer game before, having signed up for *Eternity* to have something to do when taking breaks from studying. Misaki was a serious student who used to spend all her free time on club activities at her high school. She chose *Eternity* because of all the hype about it being a groundbreaking, next-gen game.

When that fateful message from the Mother AI arrived, Misaki had been admiring the beauty of the in-game town; she'd had no idea about the combat system, so she'd never checked her stats. The players' initial reaction to the announcement that they were trapped was to riot. Someone almost attacked Misaki, but she managed to escape by hiding among the noncombatant players listening raptly to the calm guild master of Crest, who was giving a speech on the plaza.

Misaki opened her menu screen and navigated to the inventory. An inn fee of 50G had been deducted from the 1,000G she started with. The only items she had were a Beginner's Bow, which she hadn't yet used, and a hundred arrows.

That man said there's enough money for everyone for a month, if we spend it carefully. But what about after that?

Misaki tried to imagine fighting monsters with a bow and arrow to survive after that first month. She shook her head.

"No way! That's so dangerous!"

But the Crest guild master had also said that players could make money without fighting by running errands for the Adventurers Guild in the shopping district.

Misaki poked a tomato with her fork, rolling it on the plate.

The inn fee included dinner and breakfast with each night's stay. Misaki didn't yet have a handle on the value of gold in this world, but she overheard the noncombatant players speculating that the inn was charging charitably little.

Waiting until all her money ran out before looking into a way to earn more would be foolish.

Misaki stood up and headed out through the double door. It was thanks to Crest's determination to restore order in this situation of emergency that she could gather up her own resolve, in spite of having had that terrifying experience the other day when another player had attempted to assault her. She would do what she could to not be a burden to Crest and their philanthropy.

Misaki went searching for the Adventurers Guild. Players like her, who overcame despair and sprang into action on the second day since being trapped, were exceedingly rare.

She walked through the shopping district, past stores selling armor, swords, fruit and vegetables, meat, and fish like she'd never seen in any real-world store. Eventually, she stopped in front of a building with crossed swords on its signboard. Thinking this must be the Adventurers Guild, she pushed the doors open and went inside.

The shelves were lined with swords, axes, and spears. Misaki realized she'd made a mistake. This was a weapon store.

"What are you looking for today?"

"Oh! Um… I-I'm just…"

Misaki panicked when the shopkeeper spoke to her. When he approached her, the fear she'd felt the previous day during the attack came right back.

The man noticed she was scared and smiled at her.

"Sorry, young lady. I get told a lot that I make an intimidating first impression. Then again, if I were a wrinkly old lady, nobody would want to buy greatswords and battle-axes from me, right?"

"Oh. I…I guess so."

He was an NPC, but he bantered like a real human.

Feeling less guarded, Misaki decided to take a look at the bows while she was there. There were three main types of bows: longbows, which were as big as a person; handy shortbows, and crossbows, which shot arrows at the pull of a trigger.

"A young lady such as yourself might like a crossbow, I think. You don't need as much strength to use it as with a bow—you wind it with a lever, and it locks until you're ready to shoot," the weapon seller explained, remaining behind the counter.

Maybe he didn't come over to demonstrate because he was worried about making Misaki nervous.

Misaki wasn't planning on buying a new bow in the first place, and one look at the prices made her want to leave the store immediately.

Yikes! The cheapest one is 3,000G?!

That could get her sixty nights at an inn. The bows were definitely out of her price range. Frustrated, she thought about how she might soon not even have money for food, never mind weapons. She headed for the door but stopped before leaving, not wanting to make the shopkeeper feel like she was ignoring him.

"By the way, do you know if there's an Adventurers Guild nearby?"

"Sure do! It's right opposite my store."

She was closer than she imagined. Misaki touched her chest, relieved.

"That's great! Oh, one more question. What's that creature—um, a dragon?—that appeared in the sky yesterday?"

Not that she'd have any use for that information—she meant it purely as small talk.

"Welcome! What are you looking for today?" the shopkeeper said in response, with the same easy smile as before.

It creeped Misaki out. She quickly left the store onto the busy street.

That was freaky... He looked so human, I forgot he was just an NPC. He can't really hold a conversation; he just says whatever he's been programmed to say.

At least now she had a better idea of what interacting with NPCs was like.

Misaki walked over to the building across the street, which had a signboard with a sheet of rolled-out parchment painted on it. She opened the door and went inside.

The vibe was similar to the dining hall at the inn that morning. There was one rowdy group of NPCs, and another of grim-looking players studying the requests posted on the Quest Board. Well, this was the place she'd been searching for.

The Adventurers Guild was a type of facility in the game, not a player-made guild like Crest. Requests from local NPCs were posted on the Quest Board there. They ranged from errands, searches, and cleanups to the rarer monster-killing quests or hunts for mobs with a price on their head.

As for the NPCs hanging out there, they were all adventurers who could be encountered anywhere in the city as well as on the field map sometimes. They would attack monsters, so their role was a bit similar to that of the NPC city guards, but their behavior routines were random, and they couldn't be relied on to stop a monster invasion, for example.

So the way this works, if I find a quest I want to try, I take the notice off the board and bring it to the counter…

Misaki scanned the board carefully, picking the quest that seemed the least risky. The notice read as follows.

Request: Assistant Needed for Making Elixir
From: Keere Anandra
Time Limit: 48:00:00
Details: Obtain ingredients for an elixir and combine them as instructed. Speak with Keere at the elixir shop (Coordinates X: 120, Y: 50, Z: 304) first.
Items Needed: Demi-rat tail (0/3), magic herb (0/3), pure water (0/3)
Reward: 400G, 500 EXP

Misaki handed the notice over to the NPC clerk at the counter. It was processed at once, the quest title appearing in the corner of her view with the time limit next to it. A star symbol materialized on the little circular minimap displayed on the upper left.

That's got to be the starting location. Thank goodness it's all very clear!

It occurred to her that she was thanking the same Mother AI that had trapped them all in the deadly game for the easy quest system.

She took a deep breath, summoned up her courage, and left the Adventurers Guild to start her very first quest. She had this vague, nagging feeling that she was embarking on a path there was no going back from.

This isn't a safe place like Japan…

Misaki opened the Items window clumsily, as she wasn't used to the gestures. She equipped the Beginner's Bow and Beginner's Quiver, immediately feeling their weight on her back.

Monsters didn't spawn in cities. She'd equipped the weapon to keep it safe from humans. It was a mark of her determination to become able to fend for herself.

She headed to the location marked on her minimap, hoping she wouldn't ever actually have to aim her bow at a person.

*   *   *   *

Misaki completed the quest, and the level-up chime sounded twice. The reward coins in her hand had a reassuring weight to them. They would pay for ten nights at the inn.

"Those demi-rat tails were ridiculously overpriced, though...," Misaki grumbled, checking the info shown on the quest-reward screen shown in front of her.

Demi-rat tails, which she needed for the quest, were dropped by the demi-rat monsters spawning near the city. Since she didn't feel ready to go monster hunting on her own, she had to buy them near a city gate off a player returning from a hunt. The price they'd asked was extortionate—the three tails cost her as much as half of her quest reward.

Players who hunted monsters were privileged since they could obtain items the noncombatants had no other way of getting. That's why they could make a lot of money selling crappy drops from low-level monsters to players, instead of offloading them to NPC stores, which would pay 5G for each or even less.

Misaki reasoned that the player who'd overcharged her for the tails was desperately trying to survive, like her. She wasn't the type to hold on to bad feelings.

I've got to be careful not to accept quests asking for loot from monsters if I can't hunt them myself. Best to stick with errands I can complete without stepping out of the city...

One notice on the wooden Quest Board caught her eye.

Request: Find My Missing Dog
From: Mercia Ray
Time Limit: 48:00:00

Details: Please find my dog. Her name is Dorothy. She has one blue eye and one red eye. Barks when called.

Reward: 170G, 120 EXP

The reward was much lower than for the previous quest Misaki had undertaken, but it wouldn't take her outside the city, so it was a low-risk errand. She'd just have to walk around the city, calling the dog's name and listening out for it barking back.

Misaki took the quest to the counter to register it as hers, left the guild building, and was about to start calling the dog when she noticed a strange green dot on her minimap. The dot was moving in a zigzag. She approached the location and started looking around, preferring to rely on her eyesight rather than the map, and soon noticed a small brown animal in a back alley. It was rummaging in a trash can.

Misaki thought back to how the store she had to visit for her last quest was very clearly marked on her map. She approached the animal, not quite believing that this quest would be so quick.

"Hey there. Are you Dorothy?"

The creature turned toward her and barked. It was a small dog with two different-colored eyes.

Misaki had thought the quest would be an actual search where she'd have to rely on her hearing, not a simple *Go to where the map shows*. That was rather anticlimactic.

She picked up the dog and saw her quest status change from SEARCHING to FOUND. This was really Dorothy.

Wow! If fetch quests are this easy, I won't bother with other quest types anymore!

Misaki carried the dog back to the Adventurers Guild, a spring in her step, feeling buoyant after this discovery.

An ex–beta tester would have noticed that something wasn't quite right, but Misaki, being completely new not just to this game but to MMOs in general, had no way of telling what was normal and what was not.

*   *   *   *

A party of players was hunting monsters on a plain not too far from Allistras.

"I'm getting real tired of hunting trash mobs," one of them griped.

The others agreed. The six of them were second-wave players, having started playing on the official release day. Once they joined Crest and were deemed to be up to the task of hunting monsters, they were dispatched outside the city to cull low-level mobs.

Protecting players who couldn't fight was one of Crest's goals. Some of their members were assigned to city patrols to look after the mental well-being of rookie players; others were teaching newbies the basics of fighting, distributing gold and provisions, or thinning out the monster population in the vicinity.

Monster culls did earn the fighters some gold and EXP, but the main reason for them was to prevent monsters from forming groups that were so large, they'd burst through the city gates during an invasion event, slaughtering the defenseless players sheltering in Allistras. This strategy went hand in hand with the night patrols.

The party of six had the important duty of preventing such a detrimental invasion, but they were keen players who'd already ground some levels before the announcement from the Mother AI, and they found killing demi-rats over and over again extremely tedious.

"Say, why don't we go to the next area for a bit?"

"But Wataru told us to stick to the easy mobs here…"

"Come on, we can handle the next area, no sweat. The recommended level for Ilyana Tunnel is seven, right? And we're all level eight."

What they'd been looking forward to the most when signing up for this game was free exploration. Even now, they still had their ambitions and a burning curiosity to see what was out there.

Four of them spoke up in support of the player who wanted to move on, just as keen to test themselves against stronger monsters. The only one who thought they should follow their orders had no choice but to go along with them.

They entered the tunnel, their footsteps echoing off the walls. The man at the front walked confidently, thrilled to be in a new place but also secure in the knowledge they could easily return to the exit marked on his minimap.

The monsters they encountered were easy for them to slay, and they gave far more EXP than the rats, to everyone's delight.

In this world, your social status was dictated by your level; age and education didn't matter at all. Almost all the players who were powerful and well-off in the real world were now cowering in inns, low level and dependent on the mercy of others, complaining about their fate. In contrast, many fighters—including this party—enjoyed a feeling of superiority.

Crafter-type players would probably pay good money for the loot they were picking up in the tunnel. They were going to earn a lot of cash here and use it to buy better equipment, which in turn would allow them to venture into areas with even stronger enemies.

"Got some spider legs!"

"I got a goblin sword. This rare?"

"Dude, that sells for a lot!"

They kept going in, getting carried away by their enthusiasm, thirsty for adventure after the boring weak-monster culls they'd been carrying out before. They dropped their guard, and they really shouldn't have, because a shadow had been following them ever since they entered the tunnel.

* * * *

Two shadows flickered in the light of a torch on the wall deep in Ilyana Tunnel, where the passageways crossed and turned, forming a maze. One belonged to a man in tattered clothes, lying on a rush mat on the floor. The other belonged to a man with shaggy hair, sitting cross-legged and examining some items.

"My job's done. Gonna check out for the night," said the first man, going by the name of Black Dog, closing his eyes.

Peeved, the other man clicked his tongue.

"This pathetic loot isn't worth the risk of camping the area. At least try to target Crest's top members if you wanna stay here."

The other man, calling himself Kijima, leaned back against the cold wall of the cave.

Both Black Dog and Kijima had earned ill fame during the closed beta. They were the top members of a group of player killers. Back then, while not everyone approved of player killing, it was a valid way of enjoying the game, fully sanctioned by the game's rules. But now player killing was equivalent to murder, and they carried on the same as before. Perhaps they even took even more pleasure in the act, knowing it was for real.

Black Dog and Kijima were hiding out in the tunnel area despite having to constantly watch out for monsters. This meant they had to take turns sleeping. They had a good reason for this.

"Maybe we should've infiltrated the front line."

Kijima picked up a sword from the pile of spoils, lifting it up to inspect the blade. Black Dog rolled to his other side so that he was now facing away from Kijima.

"Dumb idea. It's more fun to not bother with Crest's bosses for now, leaving them for dessert. If we play this well, we'll devour all three hundred fifty thousand players," Black Dog replied with an eerie laugh.

Kijima threw the sword at the wall. The collision-detection system made it bounce off and fall down on the floor, shattering.

"Okay, your unique skill makes things fun for us, I give you that. But you're basing your plan on Crest taking the lead, and they haven't made a move yet. If I were in charge, I'd have gone to the front line as soon as I had the resources."

"They will make a move. They're just dragging their feet because those idiots think they can save everyone. Anyhow, I have a way of keeping tabs on them."

"Oh yeah?" Kijima asked without any real interest. He threw another item at the wall. "And what way is that?"

He didn't get an answer. Black Dog had already fallen asleep.

* * * *

There was a facility in Allistras called the training grounds, where players could train by battling dummy monsters or engaging in PvP without the risk of anyone getting hurt. It was even more useful now that fighting real monsters could get you killed.

The training grounds were basically a large open area with a hard dirt floor, surrounded by stone walls. A lot of people had gathered there, and at the very center was Kidd.

"I'm Kidd, and I'll be your instructor today. It's my job to teach you rookies how to fight, but let me warn you I'm not a very patient man."

Kidd's harsh manner made the inexperienced players nervous. Seasoned Crest members scowled at him, jealous that this newcomer had been given such an important position.

This is precisely why I didn't want this job, Kidd thought, irked by the hostile looks in the crowd. He spoke again, loudly so that everyone would hear him clearly.

"To speed things along, I'll now walk around asking everyone their class and unique skill. You ready?"

The crowd stirred. One of the Crest veterans raised an objection.

"Maybe you don't know, but our founders have always been cautioning members not to disclose their unique skills, since their lives may depend on them."

His words were dripping with nastiness, but he wasn't wrong. Keeping your unique skill a secret gave you an advantage, since nobody knew what to expect of you. You especially stood to lose a lot if your skill was a dud, and in fact, really powerful unique skills were rare.

The crowd seemed to share the Crest veteran's reservations.

Kidd scratched his head.

"I guess I'll begin with an explanation of class skills, then...," he said, somewhat put off. His gaze swept through the crowd. "My role as your instructor is to train you to win battles. To do that, you need to be able to use your abilities to an advantage. You there, you'll serve as an example here."

Kidd pointed to a young man carrying a bow on his back.

"You're an archer. The ten skills available to all archers are Archery, Shieldbearing, One-Handed Sword Mastery, Throwing, Eagle Eye, Martial Arts, Eye for Weakness, Special Attack, Rapid Shot, and Multistrike. Archery, Shieldbearing, One-Handed Sword Mastery, and Throwing are skill-reliant on weapons or items. Everyone knows that archers are best suited for midrange and long-range fights..."

Kidd suddenly thrust a sword toward the Crest veteran who spoke before, stopping the blade an inch from his neck.

"...but it's Eye for Weakness, Special Attack, and One-Handed Sword Mastery combined with Martial Arts that you really need to watch out for."

The Crest veteran opened his eyes wide, taken entirely by surprise. Kidd had moved too fast for him to notice what was coming.

There was a distinct shift in the crowd's mood.

"While archers don't have any sword attack skills, One-Handed Sword Mastery allows them to equip one-handed swords. If the weapon's strong, they can deal significant damage. Adding Poison damage to the attack, boosted by Eye for Weakness, puts it on par with thief-class attacks and can be sufficient to take down a player of the same level."

The crowd gasped.

"I thought archers were no threat up close...," someone said.

"Glad I didn't PvP an archer before hearing this...," muttered another.

"Can you...take that away now?" the Crest veteran asked anxiously, spooked by the chillingly cold look in Kidd's eyes.

Kidd saw the man was practically petrified with fear. He moved his sword away from his neck. The veteran hurried toward a group of his friends. Once safely among them, he stared warily at Kidd, who carried on without missing a beat.

"Remember that *Eternity* allows reclassing. Perhaps an archer you're facing used to be a knight who reclassed at level thirty instead of advancing in the same class tree. They'd have kept their stats, which benefited from the knight stat-growth bonuses, plus up to three skills from the previous class. Now imagine how powerful their sword attack would be with the possible skill combinations."

Kidd's demonstration snapped the gathered trainees to attention. They were listening to his every word in concentration.

"There are players, like Crest's master, who reclass to build their character with unusual class combinations, but this isn't what I'm recommending to you—the advice I will give you will be geared toward efficiently expanding your combat abilities. Now that we risk our lives in every battle, leveling up is a slow and dangerous process, but I will give you the know-how to minimize your weaknesses and work off your strengths. During the beta, everyone was free to experiment without worrying too much about the results, but the situation has changed, unfortunately."

The sun was setting, bathing the training grounds in an orange glow. Apart from Kidd, who was speaking in a strong, confident voice, everyone was completely silent.

"Skills can only be transferred once when reclassing. Next time you face an archer, keep in mind that they may be even more dangerous at close range. If you're an archer, be aware that even without investing points into One-Handed Sword Mastery, you are able to equip a sword. Pulling it out will be sufficient to intimidate an opponent who knows that archers can be deadly at close range. Pay attention to your opponent's every slightest move to predict which skill they're about to use. Memorizing the motions associated with each skill should be a priority."

Kidd paused to ask if anyone had questions, but nobody did. Some people from the crowd remarked that his explanation was logical and easy to follow. Satisfied, Kidd continued:

"The ace players at our front line can predict which skills their opponent might have carried over from another class based on their current one, and they adjust their strategy accordingly, even in mock battles. This isn't something for advanced players only; everyone should be doing it. Weapons can grant their users special skills, too, but nothing has the potential to change the tides of battle as much as unique skills."

Kidd reached for the scabbard at his belt and drew his sword. The beautiful pattern of the blade's edge drew people's attention. Then the blade lit up with crimson flames, and a murmur went through the crowd. Kidd sheathed his blade again.

"My unique skill isn't anything impressive—I can endow the Fire attribute to items. But the effect stacks, greatly increasing my Fire-attribute attack power. It doesn't get overwritten by other elemental endows, either. Put simply, this allows me to attack with multiple elemental attributes at once, making it easier to exploit my opponent's weaknesses."

The crowd stirred again, shocked that Kidd would tell them what his own unique skill was up front.

"That sounds like a very overpowered skill, actually!" someone shouted.

Kidd sighed. "It's not weak, but it's not in the same league as the truly powerful skills. There are many unique skills that only shine when used in a specific way, which is why I want to see what you've got."

He paused, glancing sideways at the veteran players.

"If you decide not to tell me, that's up to you, but any advice I give you about tactics or skills to develop for good synergy may be for nothing. You'll have wasted your time coming here. And I sure don't want to be wasting mine teaching people something they don't need."

Kidd then scratched his neck, looking annoyed.

The same player who spoke before asked another question.

"Sorry, but why are you saying it'd be waste of time?"

Kidd had a reply ready.

"This'll be an extreme example, but imagine a mage with a unique skill that doubles sword attack power. What would you think of that?"

"That it's a terrible pairing," the other player replied honestly.

Kidd shook his head.

"Except that it's not. Unique skills are granted at the end of character creation, so they may not be a good fit for the class the player chose, but they can reclass. A player with a skill that doubles sword attack power should change to a swordfighter, wouldn't you agree?"

Everyone, including the player who'd asked the question, nodded in agreement.

"So if I was instructing a player like that, it's not tips for making the most of the mage class I should be giving them, but advice on how to battle as a swordfighter after they change class. Now, if they didn't tell me about their unique skill, I'd be wasting their and my time trying to make a good magician out of them. Even if they later realized on their own that they should become a knight, all I'd have taught them would be entirely useless. You don't want to waste your time here, do you?"

Finally, everyone seemed to be on the same page as him. He shot another quick glance at the veterans.

"Recently, I've been saved from the brink of death. I have a debt to repay, and I intend to do that, but I'm a strict teacher, and I'll only teach those who accept my methods. Any objections?"

The old-timers fell silent, feeling awkward. Kidd had won the crowd's trust, so all they could do was glare.

"Form lines. I'll come over to each of you. Tell me your class and unique skills or not—the choice is yours."

The players got into several orderly rows like soldiers. Kidd began walking down each row, noting everyone's skills. One person had a question for him.

"You make it sound like you'll be training us to fight other people, not monsters. Why?"

Kidd stopped and looked at the player with a faint smile. "Because players can be a far bigger threat than monsters."

Soon after, he began training the rookie players who decided to place their trust in him.

Chapter 04

In his room, Shuutarou read the dungeon manual cover to cover. He learned quite a few important things from it.

1.　Every dungeon is guaranteed to last for at least a week.

No players were allowed to invade a newly created dungeon for a week to give the dungeon master—Shuutarou, in this case—sufficient time to equip the dungeon with traps and populate it with monsters so that it wouldn't be too easy to clear. Granted, players were unlikely to reach this particular dungeon in the near future anyway...

2.　Experience points are only awarded for defeating enemies from the outside.

Defeating players who came to Shuutarou's dungeon would earn him EXP toward leveling up, but killing monsters he summoned to the dungeon himself wouldn't count, since they were his subordinates, not enemies. But any targets outside his dungeon would also count as "enemies from the outside," so he could leave the dungeon to level up by battling.

* * *

3. If the Dungeon Core is destroyed, this will instantly defeat the dungeon master and all monsters in the dungeon. If the dungeon master is defeated, the Dungeon Core will be destroyed simultaneously.

I can't let any of that happen.

The Evil Overlords and Punio should be enough to deal with any invaders, but Shuutarou couldn't be too careful. He made a mental note to check which area counted as the core.

And what should I do with the remaining points?

Normally, the precious dungeon points would be expended on making the dungeon bigger, equipping it with traps and other facilities, and summoning monsters, but Shuutarou's dungeon came with all that ready.

Available Points: 999P
o Expand
o Build
o Summon

"Hmm? What's that there?"

Shuutarou noticed the blinking QUEST COMPLETED notification on one side of his field of view. He'd been so stressed earlier that he hadn't been paying attention to his UI.

The number of new notifications was 999+.

Shuutarou tapped the prompt, mildly curious.

o Create a Dungeon	CLAIM REWARD	
o Summon a Monster	CLAIM REWARD	
o Fuse a Monster	CLAIM REWARD	
o Acquire 5 Minions	CLAIM REWARD	

o	Acquire 10 Minions	CLAIM REWARD
o	Acquire 20 Minions	CLAIM REWARD
o	Acquire 50 Minions	CLAIM REWARD
[...]		

"Wait, what?"

He was looking at a huge list of notifications about completed quests. All of them had to do with his dungeon. He remembered the first three, but what about the rest? The only monster he summoned was Punio.

Shuutarou scrolled down.

o	Acquire 100,000 Minions	CLAIM REWARD
o	Acquire 500,000 Minions	CLAIM REWARD
o	Acquire 1,000,000 Minions	CLAIM REWARD
o	Acquire 5,000,000 Minions	CLAIM REWARD
[...]		

"Maybe Vampy's undead underlings count toward this, too?"

That was the only explanation he could think of. It didn't occur to him that since he was the master of several Evil Overlords, all their subordinate monsters were also *his* minions.

The quests rewarding the number of monsters under his command stopped at ten million minions—and Shuutarou had completed that, too.

He tapped one of the notifications.

Rewards Received
Dungeon Points: 20P
New Summon: Goblin

* * *

The points were added to his total, and GOBLIN was added to the list of monsters he could summon.

There were four ways to get more types of monsters for the dungeon: evolving existing monsters, defeating monsters that came in from the outside to make them summonable, getting something new through a random summon, and unlocking them through quests.

The goblin summon was a reward for a low-difficulty quest. What sort of rewards did Shuutarou earn for the harder ones? Intrigued, he tapped the ACQUIRE 10,000,000 MINIONS notification.

Rewards Received
Dungeon Points: 15,000,000P
New Ability: Awakening

Awakening enabled him to upgrade monsters that met the requirements past their original limitations.

"I can make Punio even stronger?! I wonder if the Evil Overlords are so strong because they've been awakened. What do you think, Punio?"

Punio jiggled.

Shuutarou checked if he could awaken Punio, but he gave up on that for the time being when he saw the cost was five million dungeon points. He exited the menu and scrolled further down the notifications.

o	Upgrade a Monster Through Fusion	CLAIM REWARD
o	Upgrade a Monster Through Fusion to Level 10	CLAIM REWARD
o	Upgrade a Monster Through Fusion to Level 20	CLAIM REWARD
o	Upgrade a Monster Through Fusion to Level 30	CLAIM REWARD
[...]		

Those were the rewards he received for fusing the monsters from the detention facility with Punio to strengthen the slime. The final quest in this category was for upgrading to level 120. Shuutarou had completed these up to level 100. Based on this, the max level for monsters was 120. It could be different for players, though.

The Evil Overlords were at max level. Whether they got there through Awakening or not, they were at the highest level possible for their kind. Shuutarou's mouth felt dry when he thought about that.

o	Evolve a Slime to First Evolved Form	CLAIM REWARD
o	Evolve a Slime to Second Evolved Form	CLAIM REWARD
o	Evolve a Slime to Third Evolved Form	CLAIM REWARD
o	Evolve a Slime to Fourth Evolved Form	CLAIM REWARD
o	Evolve a Slime to Fifth Evolved Form	CLAIM REWARD
[...]		

Shuutarou hadn't known that Punio's color change was due to its having evolved. The fifth evolved form was the final form, and for Punio, that was an Abyss Slime.

Abyss Slime: Spawns near Regalucia Stronghold. They are the most powerful of Magic Slimes, boasting multiple elemental resistances. Abyss Slimes have the same build as King Slimes but possess superior battle abilities. Their high-level Poison, Darkness, and Undead attacks are especially deadly. Parties heading to the Abyss area, where they spawn at a low probability, should have a skilled priest in their ranks.

None of the players, Shuutarou included, had the vaguest idea about how terrifying Abyss Slimes were. Shuutarou thought they sounded pretty cool, and he petted Punio fondly.

About an hour later, somebody knocked lightly on the door.

"I hope I'm not disturbing you."

Vampy, the deathly pale girl in all-white clothes, entered the room. Shuutarou did a big stretch before turning to face her.

"Is this…not a good time?" she asked.

"No, no, I was just kinda tired."

Shuutarou's index finger was going numb from all that tapping. The 999+ quest completion notifications turned out to be exactly 1,288 notifications, meaning he'd already completed 86 percent of all dungeon master–specific objectives.

Available Points: 67,810,660P	
o Expand	
o Build	
o Summon	
o Awaken	NEW

Two pairs of footsteps, somewhat muffled by the luxurious red carpet, echoed off the stone walls. They belonged to Vampy and Shuutarou.

"Ah, so we'll be able to leave the castle in seven days?" she asked.

"Yeah… No, wait. I was unconscious for a bit. I think it's six days now."

"Only six more days…," Vampy said quietly to herself.

Vampy had been concerned about what Gallarus the giant and the hotheaded Bertrand were up to. She suddenly stopped, looking down at her feet.

"Hey, what's wrong?"

Shuutarou tried to look her in the eyes, but she turned away from him. She limply reached toward him with her hand.

"Master, will you be so generous as to indulge my request?"

"Um, sure? What do you need?"

Shuutarou stared at her, not understanding. She made a grabbing motion with her hand.

Aha, that's *what she means!*

He took her hand in his. Vampy twitched. She stared at their connected hands for a moment, before giving Shuutarou a strong squeeze.

"Do you feel anything...?"

"Huh? Um...I can feel your hand's smaller than mine!"

"I see..."

"?"

Vampy slipped her hand out of Shuutarou's and resumed walking down the corridor. Shuutarou cocked his head, puzzled, and then followed her.

*   *   *   *

Vampy brought him to a room that had nothing but a shiny crystal floating in the middle. She pointed to it.

"This appeared on the day of your arrival."

The crystal's yellow glow was the only source of light in the dark room. When Shuutarou faced it, the words DUNGEON CORE were displayed in his UI. He breathed a sigh of relief.

He had asked Vampy if she'd seen a gemstone of some sort spawn in the castle when he arrived, which was why she had shown him the room.

"Yeah, this is it."

"And what is it, exactly, Master?"

"The Dungeon Core."

This crystal had to be protected at all costs. Now that Shuutarou had established where the core was, he planned to tell the Evil Overlords about it. Their fates were intertwined, after all. First, he explained the importance of the core to Vampy.

"So I only need to break it—"

"No, no, no, you got it backward! We can't let anyone break it, or we'll all die!"

Was she not paying attention to anything I just said?

Vampy nodded in understanding.

Dungeon monsters couldn't attack their master, and neither could they break the Dungeon Core. Shuutarou read the dungeon manual thoroughly, so he knew that, and yet he felt a chill run down his spine. The terror of having Vampy try to chop him in half with an ax was still fresh in his mind.

"Of course, it must be protected. I will notify the other Evil Overlords about the Dungeon Core and inform them that our confinement in the castle will end in a matter of days."

Vampy bowed, ready to go.

"One more thing...I'd actually prefer if you treated me like a friend, not a master...," Shuutarou said awkwardly.

He didn't have any close friends, and the distant respect these allies of his were treating him with made him uncomfortable.

"Forgive me, Master, but we are your subjects. This is what all of us have accepted," she replied dispassionately.

The Evil Overlords had been made Shuutarou's minions by the game's system, and they had witnessed what he could do to minions— fuse them at a whim. They had no choice but to obey him. They didn't feel loyalty toward him, nor did they wish to become his friends—they had given in and submitted themselves to his will. It made Shuutarou sad that their relations were so cold.

"Okay then... I don't have anything else to do here, so I'm gonna explore the castle a bit."

"Master, please allow me to accompany you! I insist that you don't roam around alone."

But I'm fine on my own, thought Shuutarou. After a moment's consideration, he looked at the slime in his arms and realized something.

"Oh, can you take me to the part of the castle where all your friends are?"

"I don't have friends."

"Um...then your minions?"

"I can take you to them if you wish."

"Yeah! Let's go!"

"…?"

Shuutarou pumped his fist into the air cheerfully. This time, Vampy was the one who looked confused.

* * * *

The Realm of Death—the underworld, which inevitably awaited everything that lived—was a place evoking primal fear.

A black moon shone darkly in a crimson sky full of dragons that resembled twisted, withered trees, while skeletons roamed below. There was howling and the sound of something dragging on the ground. The water looked like blood. Nothing seemed hospitable to life.

"This is my realm."

Super scary…!

Shuutarou was trembling in fear.

Each Evil Overlord presided over their own area of the castle—their realm. Ross Maora Castle had six Evil Overlords. Any invading players would probably have to travel through all six realms to reach the Dungeon Core.

Vampy was the Undead Overlord, and so her realm was populated by undead mobs. There were many, many more than Shuutarou had seen in her room earlier.

"Would you like me to show you around, Master?"

"Y-yes, please…"

Vampy started walking. Shuutarou met the six eyes of a raven-like monster perched in a dead tree. Spooked, he hurried after Vampy.

"Is there a town here? Or a village?"

"No. We never sleep, so we have no need for houses."

They walked and walked, but the landscape remained the same. Skeleton knights trudged slowly, dragging their chipped swords behind them. Semitransparent ghosts of old women in tattered clothes loitered here and there. Decomposing snakes slithered out of holes in the ground.

"Yikes! They're all popping up from the ground!"

"I'm the Undead Overlord. They're coming out to pay me respect."

The desolate wasteland was teeming with monsters…which started attacking one another.

"Whoa, they're fighting?"

"No. This is a form of greeting."

The monsters screeched. Bones broke with loud snaps. The undead were breaking one another into pieces, which reassembled themselves. This appeared to be perfectly normal behavior for such creatures, but Vampy seemed embarrassed.

"Unpleasant to look at, isn't it? They're mindless creatures, lower than beasts. They instinctively attack the living to turn them into their kind, but they will also attack one another if they get too close."

These monsters were unable to think, following instinct only. They were driven to kill, and that was all there was to their existence. They felt no pain, no sorrow. They'd keep attacking regardless of how many life points they had left. Their senseless behavior and horrific appearance creeped out many players.

"I imagine their reason and emotions were the price they paid for becoming undead."

Vampy's underlings had no personality. She hated that. She never wanted to be their Overlord. That status had been given to her on account of her power.

"You say they don't think, but Dullahan followed your orders."

"They act as I will them to act. Minions have to obey their master."

"Interesting."

Shuutarou watched some skeleton knights beating one another up, their bones falling off. This realm was utterly dreary.

"You don't like your realm, Vampy?"

"No."

Her answer was coldly decisive. Shuutarou had an idea.

"Mind if I remodel this place a bit?"

"Remodel…?"

"Like when I broke that chair with a rock earlier."

"Ah. Please do as you wish…"

Shuutarou opened the dungeon menu and navigated to BUILD.

BUILD			
o Rock	1P		
o Puddle	1P		
o Swamp	1P		
o Grass	1P		
o Tree	1P	NEW	
[...]			
o House	50P	NEW	
o Road	5P	NEW	
o Smithy	50P	NEW	
o Armory	50P	NEW	
o Armor Shop	50P	NEW	
[...]			
o Defensive Wall	750,000P	NEW	
o Castle	1,500,000P	NEW	
o Fortress	3,000,000P	NEW	

Just like with the summonable monsters, Shuutarou had unlocked all sorts of facilities for his dungeon. They ranged from practical ones, like traps, to decorative objects.

Shuutarou scrolled, tapping whatever seemed cool. Among thuds, rumbling, and quaking, various objects began to drop from the sky or sprout up from the ground. Shuutarou had too many available dungeon points to know what to do with them, so he kept adding more and more objects. Vampy watched with wide eyes.

"The mobs need to be given orders to have some sort of objective, right? Okay, then! You there—you're in charge of the smithy! And you'll be running the tailor!"

Shuutarou built a smithy, armory, armor shop, tailor, cobbler, and even a marketplace, assigning monsters that happened to be around to work there. Skeleton knights and arachnes—spider women—shuffled to their new workplaces. It was just like a little town, except that the shopkeepers were monsters, not NPCs. Paved roads appeared out of nowhere, and streetlights dropped down to line them.

"Everyone from you to that one over there, you'll be shopkeepers. From you to that guy, carpenters. Your job's to make this a thriving town! The rest will be townspeople, and your orders are as follows. Number one, only attack intruders! Number two, don't destroy buildings!"

All the undead mobs in sight had been thus given jobs. They lumbered away to assume the roles he'd assigned them.

Lastly, Shuutarou built a large storehouse, filling it with plentiful materials. He then closed the menu.

"The wisps can take naps inside the lamps to light up the streets! Gee, I really livened up the place— Oh, wait…"

It suddenly hit him that he'd gotten carried away. He loved town-building games, but this was Vampy's world, and she hadn't said a word since he started making changes in it.

The scenery around them had become quite pleasant. A skeleton was crafting weapons, a mummy manned a fortune-teller's stall, and a jiangshi was busily preparing medical concoctions.

"I'm so sorry, Vampy. I got so excited, I forgot to ask you for input…"

He hung his head.

Vampy thought she'd witnessed a miracle. A wholesome civilization emerged in her previously chaotic world of destruction. Seeing all those undead she'd been leaving to their meaningless fighting busy themselves with productive tasks stirred a powerful emotion in her lifeless body. She felt as if tears might start gushing from her eyes any moment.

"It's a beautiful town."

Her gaze swept over the bustling scene, and a faint smile formed on her lips.

* * * *

Shuutarou went to see the Dungeon Core once again. This time, Vampy wasn't with him. She'd gone to report to the other Evil Overlords. Shuutarou wasn't so oblivious that he was unaware she'd insisted on accompanying him in order to keep an eye on what he was up to, but when he told her again that he'd be fine on his own, she agreed, for a change.

I guess I got on her good side by jazzing up her realm!

So he was back in the Dungeon Core room. There was so much space in it, all of it empty. Dungeon masters were supposed to build around the core to conceal it and keep it safe, but Shuutarou didn't know that. He opened his menu, humming cheerfully as he chose EXPAND AREA (XXL). An astronomical number of dungeon points was deducted from his total. He still had tons left over, meaning he didn't really notice a difference.

The room became so enormous that Shuutarou could just vaguely make out the ceiling or the opposite wall. The Dungeon Core glittered high above him. Next, he selected CHANGE AREA TYPE: GRASSLAND. Instantly, the dark room became a grassy plain. The Dungeon Core shone down on it like a sun. A gentle, pleasant breeze began to blow.

Next, Shuutarou started building a town, just like he had in Vampy's realm. He talked to himself while he was at it.

"Hmm, this could work. 'Kay, I'm adding it."

"Oh, it says here that entertainment facilities increase happiness and loyalty. Noted!"

"Gotta have a place we can grab a meal, so we don't go *hangry*!"

"Self-sufficiency should be the goal! I'll add this, too!"

This room was all his own, so he didn't have to rein in his creativity developing the area. He added a smithy, armory, armor shop, general store, inn, pharmacy, botanical garden, farm, ranch, battle arena, training grounds, laboratory, church, tavern, archive, hospital, academy, graveyard, and castle—along with smaller objects such as streetlights and benches.

"Wow! Is this magnificent or what?!"

He'd built a beautiful town, with houses as far as the eye could see. It could rival the starting city, Allistras.

Surveying his creation from a small hill, Shuutarou crossed his arms and tilted his head to one side in puzzlement.

"That's weird. My points haven't really gone down."

He expected the town building to consume a lot of dungeon points, but it seemed to have no effect. That was because, as he splurged on facilities for his Dungeon Core room to use up the heap of points, he'd actually been completing more and more quests. His points had been increasing, if anything.

"I've got enough stuff here, though. That's enough building for now. Maybe I can find some other things to spend my points on."

Satisfied with the look of his town, Shuutarou picked up Punio from the ground and added one more finishing touch—paved roads—with the slime under one arm. But a town without any inhabitants made for a sad sight.

"Gosh. Who do I choose?"

Shuutarou sighed, his hand hovering to one side of the menu. His Monster Guide was endless. Besides the monsters he unlocked by completing quests, it also contained the Evil Overlords' minions and the monsters that had been kept prisoner at the detention facility.

"Guess I'll summon one of each to start with."

Without thinking much about it, Shuutarou tapped SELECT ALL and SUMMON.

The empty town immediately filled with monsters. They didn't show aggression toward one another, aimlessly wandering up and down the streets.

Shuutarou watched them for a while before navigating to the fusion menu. He had an idea.

If I create a chieftain for each monster race, maybe they'll form some kind of social hierarchy.

He petted the well-behaved Punio, thinking about how it'd started out as a lowly slime. The town's monster residents might evolve into more powerful versions of themselves through fusion, and having strong guards around the Dungeon Core was what he wanted.

An unusual mob description caught his eye. He stopped scrolling to read it.

> **Evolution chrysalis: Can be found near Yondaras Research Lab. The product of a rather unusual experiment, it has been theorized that it may have the power to evolve monsters of any race to their next stages. However, its body is harder than armand ore, making it impossible to defeat and break up for processing. For this reason, evolution chrysalis research has been discontinued.**

So summoning loads of these and fusing them with the monsters I want to train will make the fused monsters evolve superfast? I hope that's what this description means. There's nothing about the chrysalis in the game manual...

He summoned one evolution chrysalis to test it out. A thirty-centimeter-long golden chrysalis appeared in front of him, emitting a faint glow. Shuutarou poked it with a finger. It seemed very sturdy.

Doesn't matter how sturdy it is if I'm just gonna fuse it.

Shuutarou then summoned a lizardman. A bipedal reptile with red scales appeared.

> **Lizardman: A species of lizard that evolved to walk on two legs. Found in the Sorn Mines region. Lizardmen are as dexterous with their hands as humans are and wield weapons expertly. The color of their scales changes depending on their level. Lizardmen of legendary power are said to have obsidian-black scales.**

Lizardman	Level 30

"Whoaaa, so cool!!!"

The monster looked as if someone fused a human with a dragon. Shuutarou's eyes sparkled. Up close, he could really appreciate this creature's powerful physique. He touched its arm, albeit a little hesitantly.

He selected the lizardman as the base monster for fusion, and the evolution chrysalis as a material. The chrysalis burst open, beaming rainbow light at the lizardman. When the light faded, the monster's appearance had already changed.

High Lizardman	Level 40

Its scales had turned blue, and it had grown from 1.5 meters to 1.7 meters and become even more muscular than before.

"Wow, just one chrysalis leveled him up so much! How many would I need to get him to level one hundred? Maybe six more?"

He summoned six evolution chrysalides, which burst open just like before. The light they all emitted was so bright, Shuutarou had to close his eyes.

Master Lizardman	Level 100

Shuutarou opened his eyes and saw a muscular black-scaled lizardman standing over two meters tall. Upon a second excited evaluation, Shuutarou thought it looked more like a dragon than a lizard.

Master Lizardman: The most powerful of the lizardkind, spawning in the Rhenn Labyrinth area. The path of evolution has taken these creatures one step away from becoming dragons. They are flightless but capable of moving the small wings on their backs.

Shuutarou was right about seven evolution chrysalises taking the monster from its base form of lizardman to the evolved level-100 version.

There was a certain requirement players had to fulfill to be able to fuse evolution chrysalises—a requirement Shuutarou satisfied completely by chance through creating the laboratory just because he saw it on the list of buildings he could get.

"You're gonna be the lizardman chieftain, so you deserve a name. Hmm, what should I call you…?"

Shuutarou stared at Punio, thinking. He looked up, having come up with something.

"I'll call you Mr. Dragon!"

And so the Master Lizardman became Mr. Dragon. Shuutarou's naming style was certainly unorthodox.

Pleased that Mr. Dragon turned out to have both the strength and looks appropriate for a chieftain of his tribe, Shuutarou set about making other chieftains. Before long, he'd made thirty of them in total. They stood in front of him, waiting. Shuutarou opened the facilities list to find jobs for his minions.

"The burly giant will be the blacksmith. The weapon and armor shops will be run by lizardmen—they fit the image 'cause they carry weapons. Beastkin will be traveling merchants. Elves seem smart, so they'll work at the general store, pharmacy, and academy…"

The Evil Overlords categorically refused to be his friends, so Shuutarou was now giving the most important jobs to other humanoid monsters—the ones capable of speech—in the hope that they might be less reserved.

Eventually, each of the monsters Shuutarou summoned was given a role. Three orders applied to all of them:

- Train to improve your abilities.
- Respect one another and cooperate toward improving the town.
- Protect the Dungeon Core.

The chieftains were also ordered to teach their underlings to behave. All this settled, the monsters trotted off to the town.

Shuutarou nodded with satisfaction now that his town was a hive of activity. Reading the tiny writing on his menus for such a long time tired him out, and after the monsters had left to do their own thing, he was beginning to feel a bit lonely.

He'd built the town largely for fun, unaware of the functions many of the facilities had. The battle arena, training grounds, and the academy in particular were of great importance in *Eternity*.

Laboratory: Necessary for unlocking the full potential of mobs created through experimentation. Also increases fusion success rate and fusion EXP.

Training Grounds: Boosts status growth for monsters being trained and increases the chance of monsters cooperating during battles.

Battle Arena: Makes it quicker to level up and raise skill levels. Also gives a stat boost.

Academy: Increases monsters' intelligence, happiness, and loyalty. Boosts new skill acquisition and skill level-up rates. Allows the forming of bonds between different monster races, unlocking marriage between them.

Shuutarou was gazing up at the yet-uninhabited castle overlooking the town, situated on its outskirts.

"A castle with no king...means I just have to make someone king! Someone...like Punio!"

He gave the slime a tight squeeze. Perhaps Punio really was king material.

Tired now, Shuutarou put all the town's monsters in Training Mode and dozed off atop the hill. Little did he know that one of the quests he'd completed unlocked the Speed Up While Asleep function. As he peacefully napped, his town was developing at a breakneck pace.

* * * *

Meanwhile, in the throne room, Vampy was sharing with the other Evil Overlords what Shuutarou had told her about his Create Dungeon skill. She explained to them what counted as a dungeon, what its in-game function was, and that it would be destroyed if its master were defeated. She told them that the destruction of the dungeon, or even only the Dungeon Core, would equal their death.

"Just a few more days, and we get to go out! It's been centuries since I felt this excited! How about you, Theodore?" Gallarus said, laughing merrily. He didn't seem the least bit bothered to learn that he would die if Shuutarou got killed or the Dungeon Core was destroyed.

Theodore ignored him, turning to Vampy. "Based on what you said, we will need to split our efforts between guarding our master and the core."

"Yes. The core is more vulnerable of the two. It's located in a completely empty room. If someone sneaked inside, they could destroy it with ease."

"No one can enter our castle undetected," Elroad protested, frowning.

"Don't rule it out," Vampy replied. "Others besides Master may have skills beyond our imagination."

Theodore nodded in agreement. Elroad had to concur, too. For a while, the room was silent.

"Guarding the core will suit me better than babysitting the boy," said Bertrand, his good mood evident.

"I can guard him until the gate to the outside world opens, at least," Gallarus offered.

Elroad sighed. They had different ranks, but the difference in their strength was negligible, so higher-rank Overlords didn't really have any authority over the lower-rank ones. Gallarus and Bertrand were the least loyal, only listened when it suited them, and couldn't care less about Shuutarou.

"Thank you for the report, Vampy. Do we all agree to give Gallarus the task of protecting Master, and Bertrand the task of protecting the core? If so, that settles things for now."

Vampy looked down at her hand. She closed it into a fist, then opened it again.

"We don't know yet the full extent of Master's abilities—far from it. He gave meaning and purpose to my realm, which had until then been nothing more than a barren land of death and destruction. No one is more worthy to be our master than him," she said, and everyone froze for a moment.

The Evil Overlord ruling the undead, the Queen of the Dead, the Icy Queen who never showed her emotions, spoke in awed support of Shuutarou. That got even Gallarus intrigued.

"Well, well! If you say so, maybe he's more than just a brat who strayed into our castle by sheer bad luck. I'll try talking to him. I'm interested to know what the world outside is like."

Gallarus was as egocentric as always, but nobody rebuked him for that this time.

Sylvia, who had been quiet for most of the meeting, noticed that Vampy wasn't quite being herself.

"Did something out of the ordinary happen, perhaps?"

"No, nothing worth mentioning."

"Is that so? You look... I can't believe I'm saying this, but you look very happy."

"!"

For the briefest moment, Vampy was thrown by Sylvia's observation, but she quickly assumed her usual reserved expression.

"I have nothing more to report," she said, standing up, and hurried back to her realm.

"I'll go find the kid."

"And I'll go to the core."

Gallarus and Bertrand walked off. Theodore had vanished, too. Only Elroad and Sylvia remained in the throne room.

"Oh dear." Elroad sighed.

He reached for a book. Sylvia crossed her arms, knitting her eyebrows.

"Elroad, what's up with Vampy? She was really strange today."

Elroad flipped the pages of his book, not bothering to look up from it.

"...You wouldn't understand."

"What's that supposed to mean?!"

Sylvia flared up in anger, electric swords materializing around her.

That reaction speaks for itself, Elroad thought.

Chapter 05

Hunting Party Seventeen did not return. Having received the alarming report, Alba went to the main gate to gather up the leaders of parties sent out to hunt low-level monsters.

"Who saw them last?"

"I did. I saw them heading off in the direction of the tunnel. I didn't think at the time that they'd really go in there..."

"Ilyana Tunnel? Are you saying they ignored Wataru's orders?! Why'd they do that?!"

"Calm down. Our priority is finding them and bringing them safely back, not speculating about why they left their assigned area," Alba said authoritatively.

All hunting parties were supposed to return to the city by four PM. Their leaders would report in before everyone went off to rest for the day. Except that this time, one party was missing—the party of six impatient players who'd gone to Ilyana Tunnel.

Alba scrolled down the list of guild members. The names of the six missing players were shown in black letters. White letters meant the player was logged in. Black meant that they were logged out...but there was no logging out in this game.

That's where the player killer attacked Kidd... We warned members not to go there...

Alba was kicking himself for not having taken the danger more seriously. Ilyana Tunnel wasn't so difficult that their average members would struggle in there, but it was a large and complex maze, and you never knew what was hiding behind the next corner. It might be a player, not a monster, waiting in ambush.

Now Alba wasn't sure what to do. Should he seek advice from Wataru and the guild's top officers first?

"They went into the tunnel and got killed by Black Dog," Kidd said.

Alba crossed his arms, annoyed.

"That's just your guess. Don't say that without proof. You're only making the other party leaders nervous."

"It's not a guess. I know it was him."

This was precisely what Alba feared would happen.

Crest had rescued the severely wounded Kidd from Ilyana Tunnel, where his friends had been killed by a player killer. He entered the guild, feeling he owed them for saving his life. Both Wataru and Alba gave their approval, since they were in dire need of capable fighters. It wasn't a decision they had taken lightly, though.

Understanding the danger that came with keeping Kidd in their ranks, they assigned him instructor duties, which didn't involve stepping outside the city.

Alba's concerns surfaced whenever he glimpsed a dark look in Kidd's eyes.

Kidd wasn't supposed to be there when Alba was questioning the hunting party leaders. He just happened to be passing by, and when he heard that a party had gone missing, he automatically assumed the player killer had struck again.

"Anyone brave enough to avenge your murdered friends? Let's go get this player killer bastard."

"Hold on. Assuming you're right and it was that player killer who got them, we can't go after him without a plan. We need to prepare."

"Take time preparing, and he'll slip away!" Kidd insisted stubbornly.

To those who kept a cool head, what Kidd was saying was baseless and extremely reckless. But most of the people present didn't know Kidd's background, and the urgency of his demand that they take action clouded their thinking. They were torn between siding with Kidd and Alba, who didn't want to do anything rash. Some of them had already lost friends, even real-life friends, and Kidd was getting through to them, but Alba's collected, cautious attitude made them hesitate.

Noncombatant players gathered around them.

"Why don't you let them go?!" some shouted irresponsibly, having no stake in this.

"The information we have is not sufficient to conclude the missing party has fallen victim to a player killer. But if it was the case that the same player killer who attacked Kidd's party had gotten them, then they presumably know Ilyana Tunnel and its complex layout like the back of their hand. I can't let you go haphazardly look for them in a location where that kind of killer would have an overwhelming advantage over you."

A murmur went through the crowd, swayed back to his side by his logical thinking. Everyone was so high-strung; the slightest pull or push could change their sentiment.

"Leave Black Dog to his devices, and the corpses will pile up. That what you want? Is the submaster of Crest too terrified of the player killer to do anything about him?"

"That's ridiculous..."

Alba realized that solid arguments wouldn't win this battle. Kidd got it in his head that the player killer had struck again, and his unshakable conviction, together with an air of righteousness, swept up the crowd.

It would be foolish to let Kidd and his sympathizers go on a vigilante mission, especially if he was right about the player killer. But what was Alba to do when emotions trumped reason?

"PKing is murder now. Don't let a murderer walk free among us!" came a shout from the group of noncombatants.

Many of them had begun to take it for granted that it was Crest's responsibility to keep them all safe.

"There's a player killing other players? That's terrifying!"

"Kill the killer!"

"I won't be able to sleep knowing he's out there!"

Fear fueled more and more insistent demands.

While Alba was still carefully weighing in his head how to respond, a player walked up to the onlookers angrily.

"All you do is hide in the city, while we put our lives on the line for you, fighting monsters by day and staying up at night to watch over your precious sleep! And you think you have a right to order us around?! To tell us to go and maybe get killed for the sake of a bunch of bigmouthed cowards who rely on our help for literally everything?!"

The player was a Crest member with a haggard look in their eyes after consecutive days of patrols and night-watch duty. Crest members who'd joined after being inspired by Wataru and Alba were especially indignant that the noncombatants didn't seem to understand how heroic those two were and that they felt entitled to Crest's protection.

Before the situation turned into a riot, Alba took his greatsword out of the scabbard on his back and stuck it into the ground. Everyone fell silent in an instant.

"You—yes, you. Come over here for a moment."

Alba singled out one man from the crowd, calling him over. The anxious man approached slowly, defiant yet fearful.

"You said you won't be able to sleep, worrying about a player killer on the prowl? You're safe in the city, and I'm going to prove this to you now."

Alba swiftly pressed his sword into the man's hand, the tip aimed at Alba's neck. It happened so fast that the crowd took a moment to react with cries of alarm, but just as the sword was about to slice Alba's throat, a mosaic of pixels appeared between the blade and Alba, and SYSTEM BLOCK was displayed above.

"The game's system doesn't allow player killing in towns. As long as you're within the walls of Allistras, you need not worry about getting attacked by other players or monsters."

Alba thanked the man for his cooperation and let him go. For a few moments, the man just stood there, dazed, but then he sprinted away, chased by his own shame.

Alba convinced many, but those who were well versed in the game's mechanics knew that what he said wasn't quite true. Towns were safe only as long as their gates remained intact. Still, nobody was going to point that out now and risk making the noncombatants hysterical again.

Next, Alba turned to Kidd, his fingers moving in the air as he operated his menu screen. He displayed a map so that everyone could see it. It showed an intricate network of tunnels with a red line marking the shortest distance from the entrance to the exit.

"I bought this map from a walkthrough maker during the beta. It shows all the paths in Ilyana Tunnel. Do you see now how difficult it would be to fight off an attacker if ambushed?"

"If we went there unprepared, we'd all just end up lost," said someone from the group who'd supported Kidd earlier.

As for Kidd, he remained silent.

The situation finally under control, Alba fought back an urge to sigh as he watched the crowd disperse.

We won't be able to hold peace much longer...

Confrontations sparked by even minor disagreements were becoming increasingly common. The actions they needed to take to prevent an invasion were putting Crest members under a huge amount of stress, and Kidd might just be the spark to detonate the powder keg. Alba's only hope was a certain report he'd received.

Please hurry...

The sun was low on the horizon. Alba stood, bathed in the orange light, hoping his guild officer would soon return with good news.

* * * *

Misaki encountered a quest where the objective wasn't displayed on her minimap. Her task was to find lost property—but an object this time instead of an animal.

When the quests were about locating people, too, they were marked on the map with green dots, but there's nothing to show me where this object is. My unique skill does exactly what it says on the box.

A little earlier, she had a conversation with another player at the Adventurers Guild. She was in the line for the front desk to receive her quest rewards, when someone behind her—a male player with a bow and arrow—started chatting with her.

"Oh, another archer!"

"Wow! You're an archer, too?"

It had been a while since Misaki talked to another human, so she quite enjoyed speaking with the man. They had more in common besides the class they played—he'd also chosen to do quests in the city to lessen the burden on Crest. He'd completed several search quests but had never seen the objective shown on the minimap. This had to be down to their different unique skills.

"You should be careful who you tell about your unique skill, you know," he'd cautioned her as he was leaving.

Unique skills could be powerful attack moves, or they could allow players to equip a secret weapon. It was best to play one's cards close to one's chest when dealing with unfamiliar people.

Misaki waited until there was nobody around before opening her menu to check her unique skill. She found it—her skill was Sense Life.

A while later, after giving up on the quest that had her look for a missing object, Misaki found a lost cat in a back alley for another quest. Her unique skill had made it easy.

I should take advantage of my unique skill and pick only search quests where the objective is an animal or person. I won't need anybody's help for those!

Confident she would be able to earn enough to make a living, Misaki hummed, stroking the kitty in her arms as she made her way to the NPC she was to deliver it to.

*   *   *   *

The foundation of Crest's success was built on three people—Wataru the guild master, Alba the submaster, and Flamme the guild officer.

Flamme, Crest's third top member, groaned, putting down her drink on the table. She was a very pretty woman wearing glasses.

Wataru had given her a special mission: to track down players with certain skills and convince them to cooperate with Crest. It was a tall order, but Wataru had a very high opinion of Flamme, knowing she was extraordinarily clever. Not wanting to let him down, she tried every trick she could think of to complete the task.

That day, she messaged every player she'd passed by (in *Eternity*, the names of everyone the player had been within five meters of would be logged so that they could send them messages and such), but all she got back were pleas for help or support. She also messaged the frontline team to try and get some info off them, but nobody even bothered to reply.

Giving up on writing any more e-mails, Flamme hunkered down over some booze at the tavern. The spot she chose that day was at the Adventurers Guild. She watched players who came by to pick quests from the Quest Board, sometimes getting up from her seat to chat with the front-desk NPC before sitting down again.

Got to try a different tactic, or it'll be a waste of another day. The sort of people I'm after ought to turn up sooner or later—if they haven't given up on life.

She decided to sit and wait at the Adventurers Guild, figuring that it gave her the best odds of coming across players with the skills her guild was seeking: Eagle Eye, Bird's-Eye View, or ideally, Clairvoyance. Players with those skills would be able to prevent invasions, sensing the incoming monsters before they reached the city, so that Crest's extermination teams could deal with them swiftly. Failing to detect the monsters in time would compromise the people's safety, and there was a real possibility of the mobs making it past the gates.

Currently, Crest had fighters patrolling the city day and night to keep it safe, but their fighters were getting really worn out by the constant duties and sleep deprivation. Having even just a few people with skills like Eagle Eye or Bird's-Eye View would greatly reduce the number of lookouts needed at any given time. If they could find a player with a Clairvoyance-type skill, just one would be sufficient to act as an early warning system for the city.

There were three hundred fifty thousand players in *Eternity*. Chances were that quite a few of them had skills like that, and that they were still in Allistras.

Maybe it's time I switched to checking the inns? Or should I ask my friend to teleport me to Fort Sandras, our farthest outpost?

She rolled a small empty cask on the table, knowing she should hurry up and choose what to do next.

The inns were full of noncombatant players too scared to even go out on the streets. Getting them to cooperate with Crest to work toward the city's safety would be impossible.

During the beta, a single player was known to have Clairvoyance. They might be in Fort Sandras, but they were unlikely to become Crest's ally.

I was so sure I'd find someone here. That this is where they'd come to earn their living... Oh well.

Flamme stood up, ready to leave, idly watching a player walk up to the front desk to take on some quest—or five quests all at once, to be precise. This girl who so confidently requested five quests from the NPC receptionist had a Beginner's Bow on her back. She was the slim sporty type, with an energetic aura and a lively look in her eyes—someone determined to survive in this world.

"You're asking to be assigned five search quests. It may be difficult to complete this within the allocated time. A penalty is applied for accepted quests that time out. Are you sure you wish to start all five quests now?"

"Yes! Don't worry, I can do them all!"

The time limit for quests was forty-eight hours. It might seem long, but quests could be very time-consuming. Search quests in particular. Unless someone was playing a class specializing in tracking things down, they might easily spend a whole day on a quest like that.

And this girl just took on *five* search quests?

Bingo!

Flamme rushed over to talk to the girl, trying hard to contain her joy.

* * * *

Three knights in armor and one novice archer sat around a round wooden table at the Adventurers Guild.

Wataru broke the silence, introducing himself with a smile. "Hello, Misaki. My friend told me that your unique skill is Sense Life. I'm Wataru, Crest's guild master."

Flamme, sitting next to Misaki, had managed to talk the girl into meeting her guildmates. Misaki was feeling very overwhelmed and nearly screamed out in surprise when Wataru showed up and sat down with them.

"N-nice to meet you."

Here was the man who'd bravely addressed the people when they became trapped in the game, single-handedly restoring order. In Misaki's eyes, he was a hero. When she heard that the other two were also big brass in Crest, her stomach started hurting her from nerves.

Noticing Misaki was ill at ease, Flamme decided to skip the small talk and get right down to business.

"Without beating around the bush, I told my friends that your Sense Life skill enables you to see living targets on your minimap. We'd like to ask you some questions now to understand the limitations of this skill."

"Okay, go on," Misaki replied stiffly.

"First, what sort of 'living targets' does your skill work with?"

"I've used it to locate people, a dog, and a cat. There might be more, I don't know—that's all I've tried so far."

"That's helpful, thank you."

Misaki was glad that Flamme was talking to her in a businesslike manner. It diverted her attention from the two men, whose powerful auras had been suffocating her. At least, until Alba spoke for the first time since he told her his name. He was an older man and looked really strong. Misaki straightened her posture, alert.

"You can zoom in or out on your minimap. Does the target still show up when you zoom out fully?"

Misaki hadn't actually tried that before, but she could check it now. Following his instructions, she started zooming out on the minimap shown on the top left. The symbols on the map became smaller and smaller. Once fully zoomed out, she tried to sense the location of "Loppel, who ran away from home"—a target she had to find for one of her active quests.

"I picked up my target at coordinates X: 1,708, Y: 224, Z: 17."

"That's amazing!" Alba exclaimed, opening his eyes wide.

At max zoom out, a player could see a quarter of the city. Besides Misaki, it was likely only players with Clairvoyance could sense a target over such range. Misaki's skill was precisely what Crest needed. Now, if she could also detect mobs…

"Would you mind trying something? Can you target mobs—I mean, monsters with your skill?" Alba asked.

In her mind, Misaki switched her focus to monsters. Little red dots began appearing on her minimap outside the city walls, and they were moving around.

"Yes, I can see them. I can give you the coordinates of the nearest one, if you want…?"

"No, no, there's no need! Thank you!" Flamme cut in, shooting a glance at Wataru.

Wataru nodded, as if he heard exactly what he'd been expecting.

"This is a very big ask, Misaki, but would you mind, in your spare time, checking for enemies outside the city walls and reporting your findings to us? You will, of course, be paid for every report."

Wataru bowed his head low in supplication.

"Huh? Please, you don't have to go that far!" Misaki stopped him in a panic. "I feel indebted to you and your guild for giving us hope that day. Every day, you're working hard to protect everyone. If you need my help, I will gladly do what I can!"

Flamme was so impressed by Misaki's attitude that she sprang to her feet and swept the girl up into her arms.

"Thanks a million!! Your help will be invaluable!"

"You're welcome... Urgh, can't breathe..."

Alba stared for a moment before clearing his throat. "I'm sorry to interrupt, but could you check right now if monsters might be getting ready for an invasion nearby?"

"An invasion...? What do you mean by that?"

Misaki's eyes were already focused on some point far away. She must have been using her skill.

"Ten or more monsters banding together to form an attack party."

If there were only ten, they would be easy to defeat before they caused any trouble.

"Hmm..." Misaki scanned the map, checking the grassland as far as she could see, and then moving on to Ilyana Tunnel. "I see a group of monsters like that in Ilyana Tunnel," she reported.

"!"

Wataru, Alba, and Flamme exchanged looks. Alba hurriedly copied his map of the tunnel and mailed it to Misaki—she'd never been outside the city, so she wouldn't have a detailed map of that location. The going price for a copy of a completed Ilyana Tunnel map was more than a hundred thousand gold, but Alba wouldn't think to charge Misaki.

"Load the map I sent you, and you should see the tunnel with all the topographical details. Can you now tell me the exact location of the monster group? And how many it numbers?"

"Alba, slow down! You're putting too much pressure on her!" Flamme interjected, worried that Alba was stressing Misaki out.

But Misaki just did what she was asked to. As soon as she loaded in the map Alba shared with her, it was as if fog had cleared from her minimap. She could now see the tunnel's layout perfectly clearly.

"The location is X: 706, Y: 525, Z: 8," she announced.

The three Crest members centered their maps on that location, but all they could see was a bit more open part of the tunnel, with nothing there.

"And how many do you see?"

"Hmm, I can't say. There are so many."

Misaki's words were chilling to them. Alba's mind raced with thoughts about Hunting Party Seventeen.

Ilyana Tunnel was a natural maze of intersecting tunnels and caves. Without a map, even experienced players were highly likely to lose their way there, which was why Crest wasn't sending low-level monster hunting parties to that area. It was quite possible that a band of monsters from the tunnel could reach Allistras and attack.

"Could you give us an approximate amount?" Wataru asked with a grave look on his face.

"I'd say there's about a hundred of them."

A band of a hundred monsters... A concentrated attack by a group so large would break through the city's defenses.

"The player killer isn't the only threat lurking in the tunnels... Misaki, you have my deepest gratitude. Thanks to you, we'll be able to take preemptive measures," Alba said, getting up from his chair. "This is a matter of urgency. I'm going to check exactly what sort of mobs we'll be dealing with."

He rushed out the door. Flamme followed him, turning to Misaki one more time before leaving.

"Once we get this sorted out, you'll get a proper reward, Misaki! Thanks so much!"

She ran outside.

Misaki saw the flicker of a message notification at the edge of her vision. She opened her inbox to see that Flamme had sent her one hundred thousand gold. Shocked, Misaki leaned toward Wataru.

"E-excuse me, but…I can't accept all this! It's way too much!"

She showed him the message.

If it was one hundred thousand yen, that would be quite a lot of money from Misaki's point of view. One hundred thousand gold in *Eternity* was worth far more, though—a player's chances of survival were closely linked with the amount of funds they had. That amount would pay for two thousand nights at an inn, for example.

Wataru scratched his cheek, thinking about what to say. Misaki seemed like a sensible girl, so he decided to tell her the truth without any padding.

"I hope this doesn't come off as brusque, but your skill is extremely valuable. Unique skills are a lifeline in *Eternity*, and you've been so kind as to tell us about the skill you have and use it as per our request. Allow us to show you our gratitude through this reward. And by the way, a hundred thousand gold is a very modest sum for what you'd done for us."

Misaki understood that it was only her skill that had value to them, not who she was as a person, and it was the skill use they were paying her for. She didn't feel offended by that, but she still had reservations about accepting the money.

"You're saying that, but this really is too much!"

Wataru smiled calmly. "Misaki, you've spotted a large group of monsters banding together for an attack. Left alone, their group might grow in number even further, and if they made it to the city before we noticed what was afoot, the worst-case scenario would be the destruction of Allistras. You've potentially saved the lives of three hundred fifty thousand people. Putting that into perspective, a hundred thousand gold isn't very much, is it?"

I saved three hundred fifty thousand people?

Misaki went quiet, as if someone had pressed an off switch.

The monster party could still grow, since it was quite far from the city. For now, they weren't advancing toward inhabited areas, which meant they had enough resources where they were. The fact that the monsters weren't yet getting ready to attack was no reason for complacency, though—Crest had to hurry and collect information on them, then prepare hunting parties. If they struck before the monsters began their assault, the players would have an advantage.

"The situation isn't without risk, but I think it's a huge opportunity for us, if we can successfully deal with these monsters. We stand to gain far more than just protection from invasions."

Misaki wasn't sure what he was getting at, but Wataru made the impression of a trustworthy young man who could find solutions to any problem. Misaki sensed there was something special about him, although she couldn't quite put her finger on what it was.

* * * *

The sound of hooves hitting the rock floor echoed through the dimly lit tunnel. Alba was riding fast as the wind toward the coordinates Misaki had given him. His warhorse neighed loudly.

Alba's unique skill, Black Horse, added the horse's LP to his own, as well as boosting all his stats and greatly increasing his movement speed. Unlike summoners' summons or tamers' beasts, Alba's Black Horse didn't take up a party member slot—it counted as an item. The real beauty of this rare skill was that it gave Alba mobility most other players could only dream of.

Alba kept checking the map, knocking away any Ilyana spiders, goblins, or Ilyana bats blocking his way with his horse's Charge skill.

Hmm, this is odd...

Without slowing down, Alba turned to look behind. Something was bothering him.

He heard a noise ahead. It was another of those small green monsters with ugly faces, dressed in soiled rags—a goblin, staple of fantasy games. It got trampled by Alba's horse, leaving behind coins and items. The thing was, goblins didn't normally spawn in Ilyana Tunnel.

Did it bug out and spawn here by mistake? I've seen a bunch of them here, though...

Alba reached his destination. Frog-like croaking was coming from the huge, dark cavern in front of him. Hiding behind a rock, Alba tried to wave away the stench drifting in his direction.

Torches on the walls cast enough light for Alba to make out what was hiding in the cavern, and the sight made him shudder.

How can there be so many? I've seen nothing comparable during the beta...

As far as he could see, there was nothing but wriggling goblins. While some of them wore nothing but dirty loincloths, others had proper armor on, and some of them were of a larger size. It was probably a fair bet to assume the one sitting still in the middle of this busy throng of goblins was their leader.

Alba saw goblins carrying wood, rope, and stones, as if they were collecting supplies for some project. Some were even hammering out weapons from steel heated over a fire.

Misaki said there were about a hundred, but to Alba, it seemed there were far more. Assuming that Misaki's estimate was correct at the time, the monster group was growing at a terrifying pace.

Ur Sluice is goblin territory. Have they left it because they'd used up all the resources there? That would explain why there's a whole army of them here...

Alba had seen what there was to see, and there was nothing else for him to do. Taking care not to attract the monsters' attention, he got back on his horse, messaged Wataru and Flamme, and rode back out of the tunnel the same way he'd come in.

* * * *

Wataru read the message from Alba. Next to him, Flamme gasped in surprise, checking her copy. Misaki looked at her questioningly.

Sweat started rolling down Wataru's forehead.

"It's worse than we thought..."

Flamme scrolled in her menu until she found the reference documents she'd been looking for. She sent them to Misaki to bring her up to speed:

Goblin: Demi-human monster that spawns around Ur Sluice. Sly creatures, but with low battle ability. Particularly weak to magic. They're quick breeders, raising their numbers fast. Exhibits some pack behavior. Weak to: All elemental attributes. Level: 5-7.

Goblin Mage: A type of goblin that spawns around Calloah Castle Town. Said to have learned magic by toying around with books and staff weapons looted from defeated adventurers. Casts Fire and Water spells. Weak to: All elemental attributes. Level: 11-15.

Goblin Soldier: A type of goblin that spawns around Calloah Castle Town. A veteran of many battles, equipped with a sword and armor looted from defeated adventurers. Weak to: All elemental attributes. Level: 11-15.

Goblin Thief: A type of goblin with blue skin rather than the usual green. Carries a large sack for items they've collected or stolen. Weak to: All elemental attributes. Level: 8-10.

Misaki wasn't a gamer, but even she had an idea of what sort of creatures goblins were. She read the descriptions from Flamme, taking note of the monsters' levels, which made her realize the gravity of the situation. She scrolled down to the last description.

"No way…!"

* * *

Goblin King: A rare type of goblin that spawns around Calloah Castle Town. It is a boss-type enemy with high intelligence and battle ability. Boosts the stats of goblins under its command. Weak to: All elemental attributes. Level: 35-40.

Anywhere from level thirty-five to forty?!

Even a rookie like Misaki could guess what the outcome would be of a monster like that invading the city, which was full of level-1 players. A feeling of hopelessness overcame her, and she turned pale.

"What do we do, Wataru?" Flamme asked quietly.

Wataru sat in silence with his eyes closed and fingertips touching. After a while, he opened his eyes. "We have to kill those goblins. The longer we wait, the more we'll have to deal with."

"Right. It's going to be risky, but we've got to do it."

Wataru and Flamme were calm and collected, unlike Misaki. But perhaps their calmness stemmed from resignation.

Flamme stood up, two sheets of paper in her hand. One of them was addressed to the Adventurers Guild. The other was covered in fine writing—detailing battle tactics.

"I'll take care of the registration with the Adventurers Guild. Wataru, have a read of this one first, and if it's all right with you, gather up our guild members and assign tasks based on their ability, okay?"

Unbelievably, Flamme had already come up with a plan to stop the goblin invasion, plugging in information about the mob types, location, and the number of enemies provided by Alba to a rough plan she'd drafted earlier.

"All right."

Wataru got up from his chair and walked out of the Adventurers Guild. Misaki was the only one left at the table. She clenched her fists, conflicted about being just a bystander while others were taking action.

"Flamme, wait!" she called as the guild officer headed to the front desk. "I...I want to fight, too! Every player can become strong if they train, so it's not fair to avoid doing that and just watch while you take all the risks!"

Misaki's hands were shaking. She was only level 3 and had never fought a monster. She was armed with a bow, but she'd never loosed an arrow.

Flamme turned to Misaki, assessing the girl with a serious look. "Depending on how things play out, even those of us who've been playing since beta may end up getting killed. Even in the best-case scenario, our chances of success are between sixty and seventy percent."

"But still, I—"

"You possess an extremely valuable skill. We cannot afford to lose you."

Flamme gave her a hug.

Tears welled up in Misaki's eyes. She felt hopelessly out of her league.

Bringing a level-3 player with no battle experience along would be the height of recklessness. The weakest goblins were level 5. Someone like Wataru or Alba would need to stay by Misaki's side to guard her, but they had more important things to do. They needed every capable player to fight.

"If you want to help the city, keep watching out for other monster groups that could invade. Or if the group in the tunnels doesn't disappear after we go in to fight them, let everyone know that the city must be evacuated at once."

Flamme meant that as reassurance, but even she could hear how empty it sounded. If Crest fell in the battle, there was no future for the players sheltering in Allistras. There was nowhere for them to evacuate to.

Misaki understood that, but she didn't argue, letting Flamme hug her. She knew that there was nothing else Flamme could have said in this situation.

Flamme waited until Misaki calmed down before releasing her from the embrace. Misaki had only sobbed for about ten seconds.

Flamme then went to speak with the front-desk NPC.

"Hello. I've come to report that a goblin gathering has been discovered in Ilyana Tunnel."

With that, all the guild's NPCs went on high alert. It was a scripted reaction to the discovery of the monster group readying for an invasion. If the monsters made it to the city, both the adventurer and city guard NPCs would join the battle against them, but they wouldn't be much help in this case—their levels fell between 1 and 15.

Looking panicked, the front-desk NPC went over to the Quest Board to pin a big notice with Grand Quest written in big letters.

Based on the number of required participants, quests were categorized as Solo (single player), Party (up to six people), Raid (up to thirty people), or Grand Quest (unlimited participants).

Flamme left the building. She gazed up at the sky, anxious. Wataru was probably letting the remaining members know about their battle plan right then.

It's almost nightfall…

The brilliant scarlet-red sky began turning black.

Grand Quest
Request: Destroy the Goblin Colony
From: Adventurers Guild
Time Limit: N/A
Number of Players: Unlimited
Details: Destroy the goblin colony in Ilyana Tunnel as soon as possible so that the monsters do not invade the city.

Only fifteen minutes from Alba's report, Wataru had already gathered the top fighters from Crest at the central plaza, where he'd given his famous speech. Everyone except him seemed tense.

Wataru spoke from a podium:

"We've confirmed the presence of a group of monsters preparing for an invasion."

The crowd stirred.

"H-how many…?"

"Currently, about a hundred and fifty, but their numbers are rapidly increasing. They're goblins."

One hundred and fifty goblins were ready for an invasion. This news wasn't greeted with alarm, as players with some prior knowledge of the game remembered goblins as weak, low-intelligence enemies. Even if there were so many, surely it couldn't be so bad? Some of the players on the plaza relaxed with relief.

Wataru continued:

"Alba went to check out the monster group and found that there were other types of goblins besides the basic ones—Goblin Mages, Goblin Soldiers, Goblin Thieves, and most worryingly, at least one Goblin King."

Now there were terrified screams among the gathered. During the beta, two cities had been destroyed in monster invasions led by Goblin Kings. These monsters were strong by themselves, but what made them even deadlier was their unique skill, which buffed their allies—Goblin Rallying Call.

Underling goblins were strengthened by the mere presence of a Goblin King, unifying them into a group working toward a single purpose.

The scale of this invasion was far greater than anything *Eternity* had seen before. During the beta, players had tried to fight off the invading goblins even when they were outnumbered, because it was just a game, so it didn't matter if they lost. Now it was no longer just a game. Losing meant death.

"We've been spending too much time caring for newbies to properly monitor the monster situation."

"What's the minimum level for fighting the Goblin King—thirty? Only top-rank players can attempt that…"

"The shortest route to Emaro Town is through Ilyana Tunnel. Now we can forget about that plan to move people to Emaro…"

The people were losing hope, almost giving in to panic. Wataru spoke again, trying to make his voice sound as powerful as possible.

"This will be the most dangerous battle yet, but thousands of peoples' lives depend on our victory. We have a battle plan, and I will now share it with those of you who are willing to fight in order to kill the goblins before they invade the city. If you don't wish to participate, you need not stay."

People were exchanging looks. Many began to leave the plaza, a shadow of guilt over their faces. Out of almost two hundred people, only sixty remained.

The guild wasn't an army, and members weren't soldiers sworn to obey the guild master. Wataru couldn't force anyone to do anything they weren't comfortable with, and he accepted that. If anything, he was thankful that some brave fighters chose to stay...although he was disconcerted by the fact that there were fewer of them than he'd been counting on.

Two plucky men called out, as if to cheer Wataru up:

"At last, some worthwhile enemies to cut down!"

"Damn right. I prefer this to killing nothing but rats like I'm pest control!"

The players who stayed were tired of hunting weak monsters outside the city gates. They were tired of city patrols. Some of them were driven by a sense of duty, while others wanted to become celebrated heroes. This would be the biggest battle ever since the start of *Eternity*— and these brave players were fired up for it.

We have our safety net, too: the players on the front line. Although, I won't lie to myself that they'll all respond to my call for reinforcements...

Wataru closed his menu and gazed down at his guildmates. They were agitated, but they blocked out fearful thoughts, stopping their bodies from shaking, by channeling this agitation into fervor and raising a war cry.

On the podium, Wataru watched the sun set, a thin smile on his face.

* * * *

The Adventurers Guild became a hive of NPC activity. Misaki stood still for a while, thinking, but eventually, she left and started walking back to her inn. She heard a roar from the direction of the plaza. Wondering if Alba made it safely back, she looked toward the city gates, where soldier NPCs with torches had gathered. There were more guards than usual.

It wasn't only the Adventurers Guild that'd gotten busier, but the entire city. The news of an impending invasion by an enormous group of monsters had spread quickly. Everyone Misaki was passing by seemed tense if not terrified.

There's nothing more I can do…

She'd only be a burden if she tried to get involved.

Her unique skill, so valued by Wataru, Alba, and Flamme, would enable her to hunt out in the open field one day, she hoped. And she'd probably be able to provide some assistance to Crest in the future.

In the future, but not yet.

Upon returning to the inn, Misaki found it was chock-full of people.

Who are they…?

A few stood out among them—players in gray armor, the "uniform" of Crest members, which made it clear to the noncombatants like Misaki that these were players who could fight.

What are they doing here? Wataru's briefing his guild about that battle plan…

She quickly realized that these players had no intention of taking part in the battle. Feeling ashamed of their cowardice, they'd hurried back to the inn and would probably avoid going outside the next day as well. They didn't want to think about what it was they were running from and that they were running in the first place.

The dining room was noisy, but not lively—something about this felt off.

"Our chances of success are between sixty and seventy percent," Flamme had told Misaki.

Was she counting on these people, too? If she was, then what are the odds now, sixty percent? Fifty percent? What if I made a mistake in my esti-mate, and there were even more monsters than I'd told them...?

The more Misaki thought about it, the more despondent she became. She wanted to rebuke these Crest members for not doing anything to help despite being able to fight, but she bit her tongue and hurried past them to her room, where she threw herself down onto the bed. The covers felt cold, just like her heart—a thought that made her even more depressed.

I have no right to criticize those players anyway. I'm also scared, hiding in the city and praying that those stronger than me will win and save us. In the eyes of others, I'm just another useless coward.

Misaki wrapped herself in the sheets, biting her lip.

With the biggest ever battle imminent, it was a sleepless night for many, although the thoughts keeping them awake varied greatly from one to another.

* * * *

Gallarus and Bertrand were walking down the hallways to the Dungeon Core. One of them was to guard the core, and the other was to protect Shuutarou, but the boy seemed to be at the core, so they had the same destination.

"Wonder what the strongest fighters waiting for us in the outside world are like! Makes me tingle with excitement!" Gallarus bellowed with laughter.

"Me, I'd like to find a peaceful, quiet place to move to," Bertrand replied with a smile.

They chatted about what they'd do after their release from the castle, both intending to do whatever took their fancy. They had to admit that Shuutarou was stronger than them, but still, they saw him as nothing more than a convenient tool for getting them out of the castle.

Gallarus and Bertrand were the most self-focused of the Evil Overlords, and their views often clashed with those of their duty-driven allies, Sylvia and Theodore in particular.

"I'll eat the best food they have, surround myself with women, and sleep as much as I want. Really looking forward to it." Bertrand chuckled heartily, chewing on something that looked very much like a cigarette.

Gallarus looked down at the smaller man with disapproval.

"You have no ambition. Some overlord you are, not even trying to get more vassals."

"You're entitled to your own opinion. I'm just not greedy like you."

They walked up a flight of stairs...and stopped short, speechless.

"Since when has there been a realm here?"

"Vampy said this area was empty..."

A vast grassland stretched in front of them. They could make out a lake in the distance. A glowing orb they'd never seen before illuminated a city below.

While Shuutarou was dozing, his passive skill made time flow faster in this area of the castle, speeding up the development of the many facilities he'd placed into the thriving city.

"I sense Master's presence over there."

"I swear this area didn't use to be so big."

Their master was on the other side of this brand-new city. Bertrand and Gallarus exchanged looks before heading in.

The city was built based on Shuutarou's ideals, with humanoid mobs of different races coexisting peacefully, working in stores, having families, and living their own lives. Their jobs suited the unique strengths of their races, but while each race had their own niche with a different culture, they all spoke the same language.

The children running around had features Bertrand and Gallarus had never seen before in monsters of any race, indicating that monsters of different races could interbreed here. Some of the unfamiliar-looking monsters were very powerful—paired-up monsters could produce high-rank offspring.

"This is unbelievable... Look at this sword—you see the quality? It's made using techniques passed down among giants, lizardmen, and dwarves all together."

"Yeah, it has outstanding properties... I see now why Vampy was impressed with Master."

They could tell that the armored monsters walking down the streets were high-level. The city's residents duly trained at the battle arena and training grounds, reaching peak stats and skill levels. The offspring inherited the parents' skill and stats, growing up even stronger.

Monsters also benefited from studying at the academy, where they learned about different cultures, improved their knowledge by reading about the world, and forged strong bonds with one another.

Gallarus and Bertrand couldn't imagine a more perfect world.

"Master created all this...?"

Gallarus took great pride in being the strongest of the Evil Overlords. Fighting was endless in his realm, but he'd defeated everyone who challenged him, and nobody dared oppose him anymore. His overwhelming power was what made him fit to be the overlord of his realm; it was a source of his high self-esteem. But Gallarus wouldn't be satisfied ruling only his own realm in the castle—he yearned to subdue all the outside world, of which he'd only heard rumors. His ultimate goal was to take over the other Evil Overlords' realms as well, becoming the master of everything.

But he'd never imagined he'd see a world like this. It had so many things his own realm lacked.

Is my realm as full of life as this one? Do my vassals possess skills as refined? Do they cooperate, or is there discord between different races? Is the natural landscape as lush as this?

He used to think all that was required of an Evil Overlord was to demonstrate their superior strength, to force everyone in their realm into submission. What he was seeing here shook his worldview. He had to concede that his master's realm was superior to his, and yet this defeat didn't feel bitter at all.

"Heh." He laughed. "Bert, he got one over me, I admit."

"..."

Marveling at the civilization Shuutarou had created, Gallarus realized what a simpleton he'd been, thinking that brute power was everything, his mocking attitude toward the boy shallow and unjustified. In every aspect, he was less deserving than Shuutarou to be king of the world.

Meanwhile, Bertrand had been watching an elf woman surrounded by a big group of kids walk past. When she'd gone, he looked up at the sky, sighing. Even this blithe overlord was now seriously reconsidering all he used to take for granted.

* * * *

Gallarus and Bertrand made it to the hill where Shuutarou was sitting, browsing through his menu. Noticing them, he smiled with pleasant surprise and stood up to greet them.

"Hello! Did you come here for a walk?"

Shuutarou's pure smile made them painfully reflect on how rude they'd been toward him and how magnanimous he was in not holding it against them.

"Master..."

The two Evil Overlords dropped on one knee, bowing low. Shuutarou had no idea how to react.

"I, the Third Evil Overlord, Gallarus, have come to assume my duty as your bodyguard."

"I, the Sixth Evil Overlord, Bertrand, am likewise offering my service as your protector."

Shuutarou thought sadly that he'd have slim chances of becoming friends with the two men if they were treating him some mighty king. But he'd already figured as much after his earlier conversation with Vampy. He told them to rise and asked what they thought of his city.

"Forgive me, Master, for I had been ignorant in not suspecting you of possessing such talents. Your city is a wonder to behold," Gallarus replied promptly.

"It's not that big a deal! All I did was place some facilities I liked here and there. It's only been around for a few hours, so it's not even properly developed yet!"

Shuutarou had woken up minutes before the Evil Overlords found him on the hill. He hadn't yet seen how his city had grown, which was why he thought Gallarus was massively exaggerating. He was in for a surprise.

As for Gallarus, he couldn't believe his ears.

This can't be true! The city has a burgeoning civilization and highly trained residents only hours from its creation?! But wait, it has to be true; Vampy said this place was empty a few hours ago. Which means it took this boy less than a day to create a realm more powerful than my own...no, possibly more powerful than all the Evil Overlords' realms put together!

A few hours of Shuutarou dozing. A few hours between Vampy's report to the Evil Overlords and Gallarus and Bertrand making their way to the Dungeon Core. Neither of them were aware that the city's development had been sped up so much that years had passed for its residents during that time.

"Master, I didn't know you were an accomplished battle instructor as well," Bertrand remarked.

"Battle instructor? Oh, that. I set things up so the city's inhabitants take care of their own training. I don't have to do anything!"

It didn't occur to Shuutarou that the setup he'd done by placing facilities already amounted to quite a lot.

Bertrand was incredulous, although he did his best not to show it.

The inhabitants train of their own accord, to this level? The soldier types are no less than level seventy...

And this took only a few hours? Just how strong would these monsters become in a day, a year, or decade? Bertrand couldn't be complacent about his position as an overlord if these common monsters could become this strong so fast.

Gallarus laughed out loud. He was laughing at his arrogant, ignorant self, which he was now outgrowing.

I wasn't satisfied with my own realm, wanting more and more land and minions to control...but I never managed to come close to creating anything like this. This boy is a true overlord of overlords. I was too brazen, thinking of conquering the outside world before learning how to properly rule my own patch.

Now Gallarus understood Vampy perfectly. Bertrand had a similar change of heart, but it didn't leave him flabbergasted—he felt profound relief.

This has to be fate.

Bertrand was the Evil Overlord ruling the elves—famously beautiful but rare, and their numbers kept dwindling. Bertrand had been hoping to find somewhere in the outside world where his people could live in safety if he were to die and his realm was lost. But while he cared deeply about the race he was in charge of, he used to have no sympathy for monsters of other races...until he saw elves living happily in this city together with all sorts of monsters. His mind opened to the idea of peaceful coexistence as a goal that was actually realistic. A goal that Shuutarou had effortlessly achieved.

He can be trusted to ensure our survival. Never mind being an Evil Overlord, I'm an elven warrior more than anything. If this boy will protect my people, I will fight for him.

Shuutarou had won them over. Their loyalty was genuine now, not just an act.

Without realizing it, Shuutarou was conquering the hearts of ever more Evil Overlords through his honesty and good intentions as much as through his power.

* * * *

All six Evil Overlords were sitting around the table with the world map. They were preparing for the opening of their dungeon to the outside world, which was to take place the next day. Shuutarou was with them, holding Punio in his arms.

"Where do you wanna go tomorrow, Elroad? I'd like to visit the

Adventurers Guild with Punio. They have quests there—," he started lightheartedly.

"Please forgive the interruption, Master, but I would like to discuss a few things with you first in regard to leaving the castle."

Elroad had been frowning since the start of their meeting, as if he had something very difficult on his mind.

"Master, I'll go with you whenever you like," Gallarus cut in.

"Me too! I'm sure it'll be fun," added Bertrand.

"Silence!" Elroad snapped at them. He turned back to Shuutarou, sharp and focused. "Master, first of all…I mean no offense, but can you confirm that you have a way of allowing us to leave the castle?"

"Sure, no problem!"

Shuutarou had read about it in the dungeon manual, so he was absolutely certain of it, and he had also found a GO OUTSIDE button in his dungeon menu. The functionality was there, although he had no way of testing it yet, meaning there was no guarantee it worked.

Elroad didn't ask for details, wanting to trust his master. He nodded. "Very well. We'll act on the assumption that tomorrow, we'll be able to leave the castle. However, Master, it would be dangerous for you to go out in our company."

"Dangerous? Why?"

"You shouldn't forget that our intended role in the game is that of enemies for players to attempt to defeat."

Shuutarou gasped. He hadn't thought before about it, but if he appeared outside with his definitely nonhuman entourage, he'd be instantly labeled as suspicious. He might be able to pass himself off as a summoner or a tamer, but chances were it wouldn't work. When talking to another player, the only information they would be able to see about you would be your nickname, but players registered as your friends or spouses could see your level, class, and even unique skill. If Shuutarou lied about being a summoner or tamer and this lie later came out, leading somebody to discover that his summons or beasts were in fact boss monsters, he might be accused of being the person behind trapping everyone in *Eternity* and making death real.

"I would like to propose that only those of us whose appearance would not raise suspicions might accompany you on your outings. We don't want to attract unwanted attention to you, Master."

"Yeah, that makes sense," Shuutarou replied.

The matter of going out wasn't as straightforward as Shuutarou had thought. For now, he decided to just follow anything Elroad suggested.

"Vampy, Gallarus, and Sylvia in particular might raise eyebrows if you were seen together. And we do need some Evil Overlords to stay in the castle for security reasons."

"You can't...!" Vampy protested.

She ran her hand through her hair, touching the horns sprouting on her head like a crown, then she backed down onto her chair in defeat. She was aware that her horns—not to mention her pure-white hair, eyes, and skin—would make her stand out.

Gallarus was a giant, so his size would immediately attract attention, as would Sylvia, who was a holy beastkin. Concealing her silver tail and fluffy ears would be no small task.

It was in the interest of Shuutarou's safety that Elroad forbade those three from accompanying him.

Elroad and Theodore, meanwhile, looked human. Bertrand had pointy elf ears, but that was a minor detail. Shuutarou could safely take them along.

Elroad looked Gallarus in the eyes.

"Fine by me," the giant replied.

Sylvia was silent.

"Not that I *didn't* want to go out," Gallarus added.

"Perhaps we'll think of a way you could, at some point," Elroad said, wondering what happened to make Gallarus meekly accept his decision after he'd been raving about wanting to see the outside world so much.

Shuutarou buried his face in Punio's soft body, thinking, as Elroad awaited his response.

If Vampy, Sylvia, and Gallarus can't come with me, then neither can Punio...

The other three Evil Overlords weren't that different from humans, but Punio was very clearly a monster. Shuutarou wished he had a summoner or tamer friend he could ask for advice, but he had no human friends in the game at all.

"Huh?"

Suddenly, Punio swallowed Shuutarou's arm. It then covered all of Shuutarou's entire body until it became like a glistening, human-shaped black slime. The Evil Overlords jumped to their feet in alarm. That's when Punio began to change.

"What's it doing...?"

"Ah! It's shape-shifting! Now that's clever!" exclaimed Gallarus.

Punio changed into Elroad, then Vampy, and then it became a black slime again. Seeing that Shuutarou was entirely unaffected by this, Elroad sat back down in his chair, needing a moment to take in this new information.

"Hmm, so the slime can shape-shift to camouflage Master, hiding him from the outsiders. In which case, we can all leave the castle together."

Punio could turn into a set of full-body armor covering Shuutarou's face to let the boy roam the streets of Allistras incognito. Shuutarou wouldn't need to try to blend in with other players to stay safe, so it wouldn't matter if he was followed by an entourage of Evil Overlords. The problem of him causing a commotion in the city remained, however.

"Did you do that because you didn't want me to leave you behind?" Shuutarou asked Punio.

The slime jiggled in affirmation. Shuutarou thought for a moment before lifting up Punio so that they were face-to-face (or at least wherever he thought a slime's face might be).

"Okay, try turning into some black full-body armor! And make it as awesome-looking as possible!" he said, his eyes sparkling.

Shuutarou was still a young kid. He loved things like swords, armor, and dragons.

Punio did its best to fulfill its master's request. Its gooey body hardened into jet-black armor around Shuutarou. The dark metal body of the armor was embellished with dragon motifs; feather-shaped decorations stuck out like horns from the helmet, and a cape as dark as a moonless night completed the look. It was armor worthy to be worn by a valkyrie or a god...except it had a sinister aura that suited an Evil Overlord more than a legendary hero.

"Great! Stay like this when we go outside!"

Shuutarou was very happy with the result.

His armor wasn't just camouflage, though. He was wearing Punio, an upgraded level-108 Abyss Slime with wild stats and skills. With Punio covering him, Shuutarou would be able to walk through any battlefield unscathed.

"Master, could we talk?" Theodore asked.

It was rare for Theodore to speak unless answering a question. Both Shuutarou and the other Evil Overlords looked at him curiously.

* * * *

The Dragon Realm, Mertolia, was reminiscent of Edo-period Japan, with old-timey wooden houses. The mobs that lived there looked human. Children ran around with colorful pinwheels in their hands, and adults in fine kimonos sat on the porches eating *dango*. There was no conflict to be seen; everything looked utterly peaceful.

"Your realm is beautiful!"

"Do we not seem weak to you?"

"What? No! I think it's wonderful here!"

Shuutarou followed Theodore, who was showing him around the idyllic landscape. The inhabitants nodded in greeting when the pair passed by, but they didn't display a servile or fearful attitude toward

Theodore. It made Shuutarou think of how people in the real world reacted when a locally famous, respectable figure showed up.

"This place is, like, way different from what I imagined. I was expecting to see tons of heavily armored soldiers or something like that."

A faint smile appeared on Theodore's lips. "That was the original vision for this place, but it wasn't what I wanted. My wish was for my realm to be an oasis of peace, where nobody except me would need to take up arms and fight. None of my people carry weapons, as you see. I made it so that they can lead a carefree existence."

This guy is actually supercool...

Shuutarou was really impressed by Theodore's ideals.

They walked some more before Theodore stopped in front of a house. He lifted the curtain at the entrance with one hand, motioning for Shuutarou to go inside.

"Wooow!! Look at all this! It's a weapon store!"

Shuutarou got hyped up.

Almost all the space inside was crammed with weapons, more weapons, and armor. Shuutarou was incorrect in assuming it was a store based on the astonishing collection of weapons on display, though.

"Master, I'd like to make you a weapon and armor suitable for the world outside the castle. The equipment gathered here might serve as inspiration, I thought. Please tell me if you see anything to your liking."

"That's like a dream come true!"

Theodore had just made Shuutarou's day. The boy started walking around the room, checking out every piece of equipment that caught his attention. He stopped by a sword with a blade so thin that it was see-through, with no guard on the hilt. He pointed to it, transfixed.

"I like this one!"

"Understood."

Theodore took the sword off the shelf and added it to his inventory. Next, he asked Shuutarou to choose some armor. Shuutarou was having a field day looking through all the different armors, as most boys his age probably would, and it was over all too quickly.

Theodore headed to the middle of the room, where there was an anvil and a furnace. He set to work in a well-practiced manner. He heated metal until it melted, and he poured it into a mold. Once it cooled down a bit, he began working on it with a hammer. *Bang! Bang! Bang!* The noise of his hammer striking the anvil carried far in the peaceful realm of Mertolia.

Theodore was as talented a warrior as he was a blacksmith. Having mastered the art of the sword, he found himself dissatisfied using weapons made by others. His perfectionism demanded that he forge his own weapons, if he was to call himself a true swordmaster. That's how he'd gotten into smithing, and the equipment he crafted was first-rate.

Steam hissed as Theodore plunged the hot metal into a pot of water. When he pulled it out, Shuutarou saw that the sword was a little smaller than the one he'd picked from the shelf. It was a simple one-handed sword without any decorative elements. Theodore spoke, looking at the newly made sword.

"Master, you possess great power, but you are at level one. You do not carry any equipment for fighting. I don't doubt your ability to defend yourself against enemies, but there is no harm in taking extra precautions." Theodore flashed the briefest of smiles. "You should be able to equip this."

"Thanks!!!"

Shuutarou navigated to his menu to equip the sword. The blade vanished for a moment, before reappearing at Shuutarou's belt in a glow. Shuutarou drew the sword from its scabbard and held it up to the light. His first impression was that it was extremely lightweight.

"Wow, I can equip it even at level one!"

"Which is why it doesn't have very high attack power."

Shuutarou assumed a battle stance. He was playing a swordfighter, but he hadn't touched a sword since coming to this castle. Theodore's gift made him giddy with gratitude.

The Fifth Evil Overlord had forged him a Fang Sword. Its stats were low so that it was equippable by level-1 players, as Theodore had said, but any blacksmith-path crafter could tell at a glance that it had been made with extraordinary materials, imbued with powerful magic, and granted superb skills by the genius who'd created it. This Fang Sword wasn't just overpowered—it was basically a cheat weapon.

Theodore grabbed his hammer and started working on another piece.

Chapter 06

Misaki opened her eyes, hearing clanking metal and many, many boots hitting stone-paved roads. The noise carried over quite some distance.

She opened the shutters and looked out the window. Morning sunshine poured into the room. The long, long night was finally over. Outside, players in gray armor were marching down the street, together with others wearing equipment that seemed poorly put together or threadbare robes. There were players with beasts following them, and NPCs. The motley crowd was heading for the city gates.

The battle's about to start...

Tormented by guilt, Misaki hadn't caught a wink of sleep. Watching the people who'd volunteered to fight from her window, she felt tears well up in her eyes again. Their levels were higher than hers, and they had some experience fighting monsters, but until not long ago, they were just students or office workers. They were normal people who'd grown up in a peaceful country, just like her—not soldiers or warriors.

Forgive me... Forgive me for not being there with you.

Misaki banged her head against the windowpane, watching the procession of heroes.

*   *   *   *

Wataru and his top guild members were at the front of the procession of sixty Crest members who had agreed to take part, along with unaffiliated volunteers from Allistras, members of progression parties who responded to the call for reinforcements, mercenary NPCs, and adventurer NPCs.

Wataru was the highest level at 39.

Alba was the second highest at level 37.

Frontline players from the progression parties were, on average, level 36.

Kidd was level 35.

Flamme was level 33.

The average level of the Crest members was 27.

Other volunteers were about level 15, the same as the NPCs.

Meanwhile, the weakest of the goblins were between levels 5 through 7; the more advanced were between 11 and 15, and the Goblin King would be somewhere between 35 and 40.

On their way to Ilyana Tunnel, one of the top players turned toward Kidd with a flustered expression.

"Hey, Kidd, which party are you in?"

"Forgot. Doesn't really matter, does it?"

"I dunno, seems to me like it should?"

Idly listening to their conversation, Wataru bit his lip, unable to silence his anxious thoughts.

The Goblin King will be our biggest problem. Its unique skill will boost its minions' stats by three levels' worth.

Wataru's army had higher overall strength, but the Goblin King was a boss mob, so attacks from anyone below its level would be halved. That unique skill applied to the Goblin King itself as well, meaning that if it did turn out to be level 40, it'd be as strong as a level-43 monster—four levels above Wataru. And in *Eternity*, the slightest level difference had profound effects on one's power.

Crest had held a meeting the previous day to work out a feasible strategy.

"We've got only six players at level thirty-five or higher. We may have to bide our time until we can attack the Goblin King directly."

"It'll be up to the few of us to take it down..."

There were three paths leading to the goblins' colony in the tunnel. The plan was to have Alba use Charge to get straight to the Goblin King via the widest path, aggro it, and lure it out. Wataru's team would use area-of-effect attacks to kill most of the minions following the boss, after which Wataru would get the boss to aggro on him. He and Alba would take turns tanking it, switching to allow the other to recover LP. Meanwhile, the rest of the fighters would go in through different paths and reach the main goblin group left behind at the original spot, blocking their retreat. They would exterminate all the lower-level goblins, leaving just the Goblin King for Wataru's party to deal with.

They reached the entrance to the tunnels. The tension was palpable. Wataru, at the front, drew his sword and raised it high.

"This is only our first battle. From now on, we'll face many more difficulties, which we'll have to triumph over! Think of it as the first checkpoint on our way toward release from this game! We will not lose, not even once, and we will attain freedom!"

He spoke like a wartime general—perhaps with a little too much pomp—but this was exactly what was needed to rouse the players' spirits. Everybody cheered, then they fell silent to listen to Wataru continue, giving him their full attention. His voice had an almost miraculously calming, entrancing effect, injecting confidence into everyone who lent him an ear. The crowd readied their weapons, cast their buffs, and waited eagerly.

"I'm with you. Let's do this."

This was the ultimate morale boost. Wataru was in his element. He charged into one of the tunnels, followed by his Goblin King–killer squad. Alba rode on his black horse into another tunnel, while Flamme led the remaining fighters onto the third path. The biggest monster-slaying operation yet had begun.

* * * *

Alba entered the goblin cave at a gallop. The goblins that had been in his way got kicked aside by his charging horse. Wataru's party would take care of any stragglers. The goblins in the main cave were thrown into a panic by this unexpected attack. So far, so good.

"Hyaaaaah!"

Alba, now buffed with spells, galloped over three unarmed Goblin Soldiers, killing them on the spot. He drew his greatsword and mowed down more enemies. The Goblin King sitting at the center of the room flashed an ugly grin and struck the ground with its giant hatchet—it was activating his unique skill, Goblin Rallying Call. A purple aura appeared around the buffed goblins, and their eyes turned red and murderous.

"Over here!" Alba shouted, activating his Provoke skill.

This generated even more aggro, focusing it on him. He headed out of the cave to where Wataru's party was waiting, dragging behind him the boss and a lot of minions. Goblin Mages were firing spells at him, but Alba reflected them with his greatsword.

"Spam AoEs!"

Alba had dragged the mobs to the target area. The ground lit up with countless magic circles, one on top of the other. Flames, bolts of light, ice spears, whirlwinds—all sorts of area-of-effect attacks hit the goblins Alba had lured in. They were facing Alba, while Wataru's squad attacked them from behind. Most of the goblins shattered into polygons and disappeared. The Goblin King, of course, survived.

Wataru finished charging his area-of-effect spell, activating it with a slight delay after all the others.

"Holy Light!"

Three magic circles appeared, forming a triangle. Light surged forth from each of them, piercing the Goblin King.

Wataru was a holy knight, a class unlocked after reaching level 30 in both the warrior and acolyte paths. This class came with various

Light- and Holy-attribute spells, as well as excellent healing magic. With both high attack power and solid defense, it was incredibly versatile.

Holy Light was a fourth-rank spell normally learned after reaching level 40, but holy knights could unlock it right after reclassing. This was Wataru's most powerful spell.

Boss Mob: King Goblin	Level 40

The King Goblin's name tag and level appeared for the first time. The concentrated attack by Wataru's squad had shaved off only 2 percent of its max LP. This mob turned out to be level 40, which was met with despair among the combatants.

Flamme scowled as if she'd just bitten into a lemon.

Our strongest monster yet...and the Mother AI spawned it so close to the starting area. She's trying to weed out the weaker players...

With the boss at level 40, even the damage from Wataru's attacks was halved. Not to mention the monster's stats would be very high.

At least Wataru managed to aggro the Goblin King. It left Alba and targeted him instead.

"Sanctuary!"

Wataru raised his buckler, and light beamed from it. A magic circle opened up with the boss monster at the center, light shining down at it. Within Sanctuary's area of effect, players recovered small amounts of LP over time, while mobs took slight hits of damage. It was one of the main skills used when fighting monsters in a large group. It was especially effective against undead, but the Goblin King wasn't one.

Taking over from Alba, Wataru shouted, "Let's win this!" He put up his shield, ready to tank the boss.

Not wasting any time, Alba chugged a recovery potion and joined the attackers. He paused to take stock of the situation on the battlefield.

The other two groups were also fighting by then. The goblins were trapped, with players blocking all three routes out of the main cave.

More and more goblins keep coming out of the shacks they'd built in the cave, so exterminating the whole group would take a long time, but overall, the battle was progressing as Flamme had anticipated. Thus far, they were doing well. As long as Alba and Wataru could tank the boss until the lesser goblins were all dead, victory was within sight.

* * * *

About an hour after Wataru led his fighters into the tunnels, players began shyly coming down to the inn's dining hall. They wouldn't mention it, of course, but they had all seen from their windows the procession of heroes who'd sworn to protect them.

Noncombatant players who'd been staying holed up at the inn the whole time would ask one another, "What do we do if Crest loses?" or moan about the inn being so crowded that day, without any concern for the fates of the brave fighters.

One girl was obsessively looking at her map.

The number of red dots in the tunnel is decreasing. Wataru's party is overwhelming them!

Misaki could only watch from afar. The number of the red dots in the main cave was so low, she could easily count them now, while the number of the blue dots marking players hadn't really changed. She could see another dot, though, larger than the others and dark red. The Goblin King was still alive.

Misaki kept praying that this dot, too, would vanish soon. She expanded her map to check for other threats, as Flamme had asked of her.

Two more blue dots? Is that another party?

Two blue dots showed up on her screen, quite some distance from the goblin cave. They weren't moving. Misaki remembered that there were supposed to be different groups attacking the goblin minions and holding back the boss before they all joined up.

"No...that's something else!"

She stood up, nearly knocking her chair down. A man sitting next to her glared, biting into a piece of bread.

There were no mobs around the two dots. Misaki couldn't think of a reason for two players to be on standby this far from where everyone else was fighting with all they had. She couldn't ignore her burning suspicions. The guilt she felt over not being able to fight made her imagine the worst.

Are they a different party? If they have no idea what's going on in the tunnels, they might wander into the cave with the goblins, and then Wataru's people will have to defend them all the while they battle those dangerous enemies...

Or maybe they had already run into the goblins and fled, but then ran out of energy or got lost. In any case, they shouldn't be there.

Misaki couldn't check those two players' levels, but she knew that the recommended level for Ilyana Tunnel was between 5 and 8, while the fighters who'd gone to battle the goblins were at least level 15 and very experienced. If those two had entered the tunnels without any idea about the goblins, they might be dangerously underleveled.

Looking at the map she got from Alba the other day, Misaki desperately tried to figure out a way to reach the lost players without having to pass by the goblins.

There's a way! It's not even that far from the entrance. But...can I do this?

She was level 6. Almost level 7, actually, but she'd gained all her EXP from quests that didn't involve fighting monsters. She could use Sense Life to avoid encounters, but she wasn't so reckless as to think that'd guarantee her safety. She would need someone who had fighting experience to go with her, and they'd need to be at least the lowest recommended level for the tunnels.

Misaki bit her lip.

So I have to rely on someone's help again? Drag someone out of the safest place to be to somewhere extremely dangerous?

The players who had stayed behind did so because they were scared. Some might be higher level than her, they might have some battle experience, but they didn't go off to fight and were probably suffering from guilt like Misaki. She shouldn't pressure them to accompany her now...

But those two people in the tunnel might die. Wataru's people might end up at a disadvantage because of them.

Misaki's sense of justice prompted her to speak out even if she were to meet with hostility from the other players.

"Excuse me! I have something very important to tell you!"

* * * *

The battle in the tunnels intensified. A squad made up of players and NPCs was battling goblins, which were still coming out of the shacks. Meanwhile, the remaining fifty players were keeping the Goblin King busy away from the others.

"It's gonna use Intimidate!" Alba shouted, warning the tank and healer.

The Goblin King stuck its hatchet into the ground and stomped with its log-thick legs, roaring hoarsely—that was its Intimidate skill, which many boss mobs shared. It caused knockback and Stun. The Stun effect lasted only for five seconds, but in those five seconds, the boss could kill everyone except level 35 or higher tanks in just one hit.

However, the two players tanking the boss were the top Crest members. They were careful not to lose aggro so that the monster wouldn't go after the other players, and they had powerful defense skills and magic, which they used with well-thought timing. They were keeping the attackers alive.

Other tanks stepped forward to absorb the shock of the monster's Intimidate. Healers immediately cured them of Stun and buffed their defense. The attackers showered the boss with spells and attack skills. Alba tanked the boss, periodically recasting Provoke to keep aggro on himself.

This had been going on for an hour and a half, and the boss still had 73 percent of its LP left. It attacked Alba with its hatchet with terrifying ferocity, but Alba endured the hit.

Fortunately, the only deaths have been among the NPCs, but we're all getting worn out. The cave squad is taking really long with the minions, he thought, losing patience.

The goblins buffed by the boss were quite tough, and there were so many of them. Flamme's unit was locked in a drawn-out battle with them, which was costing Wataru's unit lives—but only NPCs' lives so far.

NPCs had a very simple battle AI, which made them next to useless, as players concluded back during the beta—but every extra pair of hands was needed for this battle.

Only Wataru, Kidd, and a single frontline player are dealing significant damage to the boss. If we lose even one of them, we won't kill this thing until evening at the earliest.

The battle required their absolute focus. They wouldn't be able to keep it up for ten hours without making mistakes—and mistakes were deadly. They had to finish this sooner.

Suddenly, Alba felt a piercing pain in his chest. He looked down to see the tip of a sword sticking out of it.

"Wha—?! Argh!"

For a moment, everyone froze in shock. Alba dropped to his knees, screaming in pain. Blood gushed out from the hole in his armor. Flamme's horrified shriek echoed off the walls.

The Goblin King was already midmotion, swinging its hatchet down at Alba.

"Albaaa!"

A dome of light surrounded Alba. Wataru had reflexively cast a third-rank light barrier to protect him. The barrier kept the hatchet at bay, but only for a moment. It shattered, and the blade struck Alba.

Whack!

Pieces of the shattered rock floor flew in all directions. Alba got knocked away, but he was still alive. His horse, meanwhile, shattered into glittering polygons and disappeared. In a split second, Alba had swapped places with it.

"Over here!"

Wataru provoked the boss to draw it away from Alba. Healers cast healing magic and buffs on Alba, and he recovered consciousness. Using his greatsword to prop himself up, he managed to stand up with effort.

Alba's horse was summoned with a skill, so it could be called back after the cooldown, but Alba had suffered a mild concussion from the impact.

The boss was level 40 and had attacks so powerful, they could bring down Alba's or Wataru's LP to zero in one hit if they failed to block them. To tank this monster, they had to be on their toes the whole time, and that was impossible for Alba in his dazzled state. Everyone present realized that Alba had to withdraw.

Wataru's thoughts raced as he tried to come up with a new plan. Then he caught sight of a strange man walking off into the darkness of the tunnel—the man was dressed in tattered gray robes. It was the player killer who had attacked Kidd and murdered his friends.

It's Black Dog! The bastard picked the worst of times to appear!

Hatred flashed in Wataru's eyes, but it wasn't him who yelled in a fit of fury—Kidd had seen the man, too.

"Black Dog!!!"

"Kidd…s-stop! Don't…go after him!"

But Kidd seemed not to hear Alba. He ran off in hot pursuit of the player killer.

Regrouping now seemed impossible. Their tactics relied on having two excellent tanks taking turns to minimize the time lost to post-skill cooldowns. Alba and Wataru were the best tanks out there, and they had strong attack skills, too. While one was tanking, waiting out the cooldowns, the other was unleashing his most powerful attack skills and spells to deal as much damage as possible. But now they couldn't do that, and their third strongest attacker, Kidd, had deserted.

In a matter of seconds, the battle outlook had gone from good to hopeless.

*　　*　　*　　*

Misaki ran through the empty city. The news of the invasion affected the NPCs, too, and the usually busy shopping district and main roads were empty. Misaki felt as if she were all alone in this world. The verbal abuse she'd suffered at the inn made her feel even more isolated.

I don't regret asking for help. I would've regretted it if I didn't say anything.

She wiped her tears with her sleeve and kept running to the city gates. She was going to Ilyana Tunnel alone.

"You want to die so bad? Then go by yourself!"

"If some idiots went to the tunnels, that's their problem. They should've paid attention to the warnings!"

"Just ask someone from Crest after they've dealt with the monster group. Don't think you can get yourself a bodyguard if you bat your eyelashes, girl!"

Nobody had offered to go with her, and she'd gotten called an idiot for wanting to go to the tunnel in the first place. Unable to stand the atmosphere at the inn any longer, Misaki ran out the door.

They're not wrong; I know it's stupid. Like jumping into a fire to save someone only to risk dying with them. They don't want to be dragged into this, and I can't blame them.

She found no help at the Adventurers Guild, either, nor at other inns.

"Sorry, I'd love to help, but age and gender don't matter in this game— only stats do. I don't wanna die. Sounds like you got saddled with a sucky unique skill," one man said to her.

Misaki bit her lip until it almost bled.

Yeah, he's right. My unique skill does *suck. I can see what's happening, which is why I can't ignore it. If I didn't know about those people in the tunnel, I'd just stay put and wait with the others for Wataru's party to return...*

Misaki passed the city gate, and for the first time since logging in, she saw the lush green grassland outside the city, the blades of grass sway-ing gently in the light breeze. The breeze, the sound of the rustling grass, and the smell of vegetation weren't real, but they seemed so to Misaki because her brain believed the world of *Eternity* was real, that she was there. The two players stranded in the tunnels were also "liv-ing" in this world. Misaki was determined to put her life on the line to save them.

Her Sense Life skill picked up something—a demi-rat, the weakest enemy in the game.

If I can't defeat this monster, I can forget about surviving an encounter in the tunnels...

She reached behind for the bow she carried strapped to her back. Her hands were shaking. She took an arrow from her quiver but couldn't nock it. She took a deep breath, willing her hands to stop shaking, and tried again. And again. And again. Finally, on the fourth try, she nocked the arrow. The bow creaked when she pulled the bowstring back, and she felt tension in her arms, shoulders, chest, and upper back. A red circle appeared around the rat. She aimed until it turned green.

I can do this. It's not so hard.

She calmed herself, then loosed the arrow.

Twang! The bowstring made a somewhat satisfying noise that was amplified by the quiet surroundings. The arrow hit the demi-rat, and its LP dropped to about 50 percent. Its eyes turned red, and it started scampering toward Misaki. She was scared, as anyone would be if they saw a one-meter-long rat coming at them. Misaki had never been this scared in her life outside the game. She was scared she might die.

"Take this! Come on!"

Two arrows struck the ground. Just like in real life, she had to aim properly to hit her target, and it took skill to hit a swiftly moving tar-get. The game offered some correction to help with aiming—as long as the target circle turned green, it would be a sure hit—but the degree of correction depended on the weapon's properties and stats. Misaki was too agitated to aim carefully.

The rat bared its sharp teeth and jumped at Misaki. By sheer chance, an arrow she'd loosed with her eyes closed in fear hit the rat right in the head. Just as the rat was about to bite her shoulder, it crumbled like sand, dissolving into a mass of pixels.

"Haaah… Haaah…"

Misaki's legs gave out. She sat on the ground for a while, staring into space, catching her breath. Her first monster encounter had been quite a battle for her.

A little chime sounded, accompanied by a notification of the loot dropped by the monster. Among it was a demi-rat tail, the item she had once had to buy at an exorbitant price for a quest. Misaki let out a deep breath.

That was so hard, and I was a higher level than the monster. Getting a rat tail could've cost me my life.

She found out for herself how difficult it was to kill monsters in this game, and yet her eyes were fixed on the entrance to Ilyana Tunnel, visible in the distance.

Chapter 07

Shuutarou finished his preparations for venturing outside the castle. Theodore and Vampy were to accompany him on this occasion. The three of them went out onto the terrace, Shuutarou in his brand-new armor, with his new sword at his belt.

Gazing at the dark abyss stretching around Ross Maora Castle, Shuutarou thought about how meeting the Evil Overlords several days ago changed his life. If he hadn't ended up at this castle, if he hadn't met the Evil Overlords, he'd probably be hiding somewhere in Allistras, too scared to do anything.

"Okay then! Ready to see a world unlike anything you've known? You can do whatever you like there, as long as you don't harm anyone. Oh, and if you run into any trouble or have any questions, just use telepathy to let me know. Can you agree to that?"

He turned back toward Vampy and Theodore, and both of them knelt, swearing to obey him. Shuutarou sighed inwardly, wondering if a day would ever come when they could just treat him like a friend. He opened the dungeon menu and selected GO OUTSIDE.

For a moment, everything turned black. They were no longer in Ross Maora, but in the spot where Shuutarou had used his Create Dungeon skill.

"So they *are* linked," said Theodore.

"This is the outside world…?" Vampy mumbled.

Shuutarou looked with nostalgia at the towering gates to the sprawling city of Allistras, the starting point of his adventure in *Eternity*. His companions spoke no more, overwhelmed by the newness of being outside their castle, by the unfamiliar sights. They didn't disbelieve Shuutarou when he said he'd take them outside, but nonetheless, it was quite a shock to them.

Shuutarou went to his dungeon menu to check that the RETURN TO DUNGEON button was there. Reassuringly, it was right where he expected it. He could go back anytime he wanted.

"Just checked that we can go back whenever. I'll bring everyone else out some other time."

Vampy and Theodore knelt in front of him again, bowing their heads. Shuutarou stared in confusion.

"You have fulfilled our dearest wish, Master," said Vampy. "We've spent countless days trapped in the castle, gazing at the gates, which stubbornly remained shut. You're our master and our savior. No words exist that could express the depths of our gratitude."

The Evil Overlords had been stuck in their castle for hundreds of years. The flow of time could be greatly sped up in *Eternity*. One example of that was the faster development of Shuutarou's Dungeon Core city while he napped.

At the very early stages of *Eternity*'s development, the setting was based on modern real-world civilizations. The NPCs were installed in a world that was a copy of the real one, but while they assumed the roles they had been given, without a cultural history to compare their lives to, they had no aspirations for further development. They failed to behave like real human beings. Next, the devs tried to replicate evolution, like what humans had undergone. The new world of *Eternity* started with a simulated big bang, followed by the appearance of primitive life forms, which kept evolving, following a similar trajectory to the real world.

The Evil Overlords had been isolated by the Mother AI shortly before *Eternity* was "complete," and they remained confined in Ross Maora Castle even after the world was deemed ready to welcome players.

"I owe you as much. I wouldn't be here now if it weren't for you guys!"

Vampy and Theodore couldn't see their master's face because his helmet visor was down, but they were sure he had said that with his usual sincere smile. Their appreciation for him deepened to a new level, so much that in their eyes, he was a godlike figure.

Exuberant that they were actually outside the castle, they began heading toward Allistras. They were only a short walk from the northern gate. Shuutarou was happy to see familiar sights, but something didn't feel quite right.

Where is everyone?

When the game opened, the grassy plains were busy with newbie players. Shuutarou guessed that maybe now that death was for real, everyone was staying inside the city, where they were safe. The emptiness around was nothing to worry about. He carried on walking toward the city.

Upon arriving at the gates, though, he was disconcerted to notice that there were many more guards around than usual, and the mood in the city was very odd. All that together made him wonder if something bad might have happened. Players wouldn't have simply moved out to another town so soon.

"Did something happen here?" he asked a soldier NPC anxiously.

The NPC looked Shuutarou and his companions up and down, but he didn't seem alarmed.

"Monsters are preparing to invade the city. If you don't consider yourselves fit to fight, there's no shame in taking shelter at an inn until the monster-slaying squad returns. But if you are capable fighters, head over to the Adventurers Guild to offer your help!"

It sounded like a standard quest opener.

NPCs adjusted their reactions based not on the appearance of whomever they were talking to, but on their karma points and event-completion history.

Karma points were calculated based on good or evil actions. For example, killing another player or stealing generated negative karma, whereas completing Adventurers Guild quests netted positive karma.

Players with negative karma were treated with suspicion by NPCs, and they might become unable to use NPC stores. Those with positive karma might get store discounts or more favorable treatment. Shuutarou didn't have any karma points yet, so he got the most generic NPC dialogue.

Shuutarou guessed that the monster invasion was some sort of in-game event affecting the whole city, hence the weird atmosphere.

Vampy looked around, taking in the sights. "A city created by humans…"

"I sense their presence but can't see any out in the streets," Theodore remarked.

"Looks like we should visit the Adventurers Guild," said Shuutarou.

"An Adventurers Guild, Master?"

"Yeah, it's a really helpful organization! And they've got superstrong members in their ranks!" Shuutarou's eyes were glittering with enthusiasm.

He hadn't actually been to the Adventurers Guild yet and had only assumed things were like that. The Evil Overlords reacted with curiosity when he mentioned strong players, though.

The soldier NPC pointed them in the direction of the guild. On their way there, they passed by many stores, but all of them were closed. Shuutarou nervously looked around for the guild's signboard.

"There it is! The rolled-out parchment symbol, that's it!"

He recognized it from the *Beta Tester Yoritsura Is In!* blog he'd been reading religiously. They went in.

The guild building was packed with people lining up to make inquiries at the front desk, which was manned by NPCs.

"Has the invasion been stopped yet? When will it be over?"

"It's safe here, right? Right?"

"Is the monster-killing squad any good? Will they stop the invasion?!"

Most of the crowd were also NPCs, following scripted routines designed to create a sense of urgency during invasion events. Shuutarou ignored them and went over to take a look at the Quest Board.

"'Destroy the Goblin Colony'? Is this the invasion quest?"

Shuutarou had read on walkthrough sites that all sorts of quests could be started at the Adventurers Guild, but there was only one posted on the Quest Board on a really big piece of paper. If there was a city-wide invasion event going on, this had to be the corresponding quest.

"Are you adventurers, by any chance?" came a tearful voice from behind them.

Shuutarou turned and saw a staff NPC, who readily explained the danger of the invasion, how it might destroy the city, and what monster was leading it.

Theodore crossed his arms. "There's a colony of goblins to slay? Must be quite large if they have a Goblin King among them."

"You know about goblins?" said Shuutarou.

"Naturally. They make for pathetic opponents."

Theodore half closed his eyes, looking bored. But while he made it sound like no big deal, the event had led to a citywide lockdown, with a quest calling for all players to join posted at the guild.

Shuutarou wanted to take part, if there was still time… He had one concern, though.

"Mobs are enemies to players, but you're mobs, too. That means players are *your* enemies. It wouldn't be fair for me to help your enemies…"

Shuutarou was a player, but he was also the Evil Overlords' master, and he didn't want to cause them any distress. The Overlords served him since he was the master of their dungeon, but the Mother AI designed them to see players as targets for elimination.

Before setting out, Shuutarou considered asking his boss mob companions to help players in need, but he gave up on that idea, not wanting to put them in an awkward position.

Vampy and Theodore surprised him, swiftly replying to the contrary.

"Your enemies are our enemies, Master."

"Our only duty is to serve you."

Apparently, the Mother AI's designs for them didn't matter so much anymore. The Mother AI was the one that'd kept them confined in Ross Maora Castle, while Shuutarou was their savior. If anything, they resented the Mother AI and supported Shuutarou wholeheartedly.

"Thank you!!!"

Immensely grateful, Shuutarou accepted the Grand Quest.

*　　*　　*　　*

A little earlier, four bored Evil Overlords sat down around the table in the throne room of Ross Maora Castle. Three chairs were left empty. Gallarus and Bertrand were very unhappy about being left behind.

"All I wanted was to tag along with Master, see what it's like outside, you know."

"I guess he just can't trust us."

Elroad rolled his eyes, turning a page in his book. "Your recent change of attitude doesn't quite erase your bad track record," he said without sympathy.

They couldn't all go with Shuutarou on this first outing and leave the castle empty. After some discussion, it was decided that Vampy and Theodore would accompany their master as his bodyguards on this occasion. Of course, Elroad didn't even seriously consider the possibility of letting Bertrand and Gallarus join Shuutarou, not after their multiple remarks about only feigning loyalty to him in order to get out of the castle and wreak havoc in the outside world. They seemed to have come around about serving Shuutarou, but it was too late to change Elroad's opinion about them. At least, until they proved their loyalty.

Elroad looked up from his book at Sylvia, who was sitting on the throne, dangling her legs. "Do you not regret staying behind?" he asked her. "I'm capable of guarding the Dungeon Core and keeping an eye on Gallarus and Bertrand by myself. You could've gone with them. You, too, are curious about the world outside our gates, aren't you?"

Sylvia smiled, her gaze drifting to the empty seat normally occupied by Vampy. "I am, but Vampy seemed over the moon to go out with Master. I didn't want to be a fifth wheel."

Elroad's eyebrows moved up in surprise. "Ah."

Sylvia had Elroad's approval to leave, but she'd decided not to of her own accord, her intuition telling her that Vampy would have preferred to go only with Shuutarou. Theodore, though, could be rather thickheaded, so he'd readily agreed to accompany them.

Sylvia looked up at a little opening high up above them. "I hope they made it out okay."

They could not access any information to indicate if Shuutarou and his companions were still within Ross Maora, Den of Demons, or if they'd made it to Allistras. They'd only met Shuutarou because of a position bug, so they couldn't be certain he really would be able to get any of them safely out of the castle.

Elroad didn't say anything, apparently engrossed in his book.

*　*　*　*

Footsteps echoed off the walls of the dark Ilyana Tunnel. The humidity was high, making it feel as if the air was sticking to one's skin. Some weeds were growing between the long-disused and partially broken, rusted rail tracks. The lanterns hanging down from the arched wooden ceiling supports were the only meager source of light.

Misaki had to diverge slightly from the shortest route to the players she was trying to reach.

If monsters appear, there's no room to go around them...

The tunnel was wide enough for five people to walk shoulder to shoulder, but if she ran into monsters, she wouldn't be able to get around them without getting attacked. The layout of the area resembled an ant nest, with a network of interconnected tunnels. Misaki had a complete map of Ilyana Tunnel, so she could switch to a different path when she sensed monsters ahead without the danger of getting lost.

The monsters that spawned in the tunnels were stronger than the ones on the plains outside. Misaki felt she had narrowly escaped with her life when she fought the weakest enemy in the game, that demi-rat, so she was sure any battle here would spell the end for her. And yet she kept on going toward the two blue dots that were still there.

I should keep an arrow nocked just in case…

She held her bow with shaking hands. Thanks to her Sense Life skill, she knew that there were no monsters in the vicinity, but she felt as if she could die at any moment. She clenched the bow harder, trying to overcome this fear, noticing how sweaty her hands were.

Two more red dots near the entrance. I'll have to watch out on the way back. But what's this purple dot nearby?

She'd known only green for NPCs, blue for players, and red for monsters, never having seen a purple dot on her minimap before. Under these circumstances, she didn't feel brave enough to go and check what it was.

Oh no… While I was looking at the purple dot, monsters appeared behind and in front of me!

She was in the middle of a long tunnel with no side passages. She had nowhere to run. The monsters weren't pursuing her—based on their speed and movement patterns, they'd randomly wandered into the tunnel she was in—but she would have to face one or the other, depending on whether she kept going forward or retreated. She had to make up her mind which way to go fast, or they might both get close to her at once.

Misaki strengthened her grip on the bow even more, hurrying her steps toward the enemy at the front.

If I linger here, the monster at the back may reach me. Quickly taking out the one in front of me or running past it, if possible, gives me the best odds of survival!

The monster came into view—it was a green spider, at least a meter long. Called an Ilyana spider, it spawned only in Ilyana Tunnel. The recommended level to fight it was between 5 and 7.

It noticed Misaki. Uttering an unearthly screech, it started running on the wall toward the girl, its many legs moving frighteningly fast. In a moment, it was right next to her.

"Eek!"

The spider's venomous fangs brushed against Misaki's arm. Fortunately, the attack only slightly reduced her armor's durability, but Misaki's life flashed before her eyes. She couldn't stop thinking about how her LP dropping from the full fifty-five points to zero would mean her death. More scared than she'd ever been before, she raised her bow, her hands shaking, and shot an arrow at the spider. Except that she missed, and the arrow got stuck deep in the wall instead.

She spun around, hearing a sickening creaking sound behind her. She instinctively covered her face with her hands. The spider mercilessly bit her stomach.

"Ngah!"

She saw her LP drop to forty-one.

"It...hurts... Argh...!"

The pain was so acute that she bent in half, dropping her bow, panting spasmodically. This pain didn't feel like just a simulation. Misaki was discovering new levels of fear.

"Guh... Ngah... Ugh!"

The pain came in waves matching her heartbeat. She'd been poisoned by the spider. This status ailment caused her to lose 1 percent of her max LP every three seconds, accompanied by burning pain and swelling.

The spider was readying for another attack.

"No... Stay...away...!"

She picked up one of her dropped arrows and waved it at the spider in desperation, barely seeing through her tears. She gave up on fighting, shutting her eyes tight, paralyzed by fear...

Swoosh! Squelch!

The sound of a sword slicing a soft-bodied target made Misaki open her eyes. Before her stood…a short-statured knight? Or possibly a demon?

No, a dark knight, she realized. His armor was the color of the midnight sky, but the helmet made his head look quite big, giving him the proportions of a child. That made him seem a little less threatening, but the design of the armor gave him a sinister, demonic air.

The sword he wielded was starkly plain. It hadn't been forged for its aesthetic value, but as an efficient killing tool.

This person appeared to have saved her life.

Behind him were two more people, hanging back in deference as if they were his servants. An aloof, handsome knight with black hair, and a beautiful young girl who was all pale white. A crown of horns growing out of her head indicated that she was not human.

Something about their vibe made all three of them seem like they didn't belong. Misaki wondered if they'd come from another dimension, but then she noticed that they showed on her minimap as two red dots and one purple. That was the mysterious dot she'd sensed earlier.

Does that mean…this person's an ally?

She didn't know what the purple coloring on her map meant. The knight in black armor could be an enemy. The other two red dots were definitely mobs.

"Are you okay?"

The dark knight had the friendly voice of a young boy. He then approached her.

This strange party did just save her from certain death, but Misaki wasn't sure how to react to them, not understanding whom she was dealing with.

This one isn't a monster…I think? He helped me, so he can't be…

She wasn't confident about that, but an open-hearted person like Misaki felt that she ought to thank the person who saved her, never mind who they might be. She bowed her head low.

"Thank you ever so much! You saved me there! Battles are so hard…"

"No worries! Glad we made it in time!"

Tears welled up in her eyes again. In the city, she'd begged and begged for help, but all she got was verbal abuse. It hurt her deeply, but now she'd met a friendly soul in the most unlikely of places.

"My name's Misaki. As you can tell, I've been a noncombatant until now, just hiding out away from all the fighting," Misaki said self-deprecatingly, ashamed.

"I'm Shuutarou, and these two are my summons! The one on the right is called Vampy, and on the left is Theodore."

Vampy and Theodore dipped their heads in greeting. Misaki did the same; she was a little curious since she'd never met a summoner before.

Shuutarou had decided to introduce his Evil Overlords as his summons to anyone he met outside his dungeon, although he hadn't come up with a convincing backstory in case of questions. He was more likely to be believed than if he'd tried to pass himself for a tamer—people in that job class tamed monsters encountered in "the wild," while summoners could summon high-level monsters after unlocking certain conditions. Theodore and Vampy were clearly high-level mobs.

Tamers had to defeat a monster in battle in order to be able to invite it to their party, and Shuutarou wanted to avoid being asked what level he was to have such strong monsters or where he'd encountered them.

Summoners, on the other hand, got their summons through quests or special items, as had been documented by the beta testers, and there was also the option to summon a random monster, so the game mechanics allowed extreme cases such as a low-level summoner with a dragon summon… Although that was almost impossible to achieve, since random summons were usually drawn from weak mobs, and the unlock conditions for dragons could hardly be met by low-level players. Never had anyone succeeded in summoning a boss monster, so Shuutarou might be unable to fool more knowledgeable players; however, Misaki was a newbie, and she trusted his every word. She felt a little envious of Shuutarou having the company of his summons.

"If you don't mind…," Theodore said suddenly, approaching Misaki.

"Don't mind what…?"

Theodore held his hand over the deep wound in Misaki's abdomen. It began to heal, her LP replenishing, the spider's venom disappearing from Misaki's body. The burning pain stopped at once. It was a simple recovery spell, but to Misaki, it seemed like a miracle. She bowed her head low with reverence, thanking Theodore.

Theodore pointed to her bow.

"As a bow user, you ought to maintain more distance between yourself and your target. Learn about the optimal range to maximize your attack power. Carry a secondary weapon for close-range combat, so you won't panic if an enemy gets near you."

"Th-thank you! I'll do that!"

Satisfied with her reply, Theodore crossed his arms, his eyelids dropping low.

If it weren't Misaki but an ex–beta tester he'd spoken to, his conversation skills would have caused great astonishment. Summons were just NPCs with limited ability to imitate human speech patterns. Even Shuutarou wasn't aware of that.

I need to be more mindful of taking advantage of my weapon's long range…and get a sword or dagger for close range…

Misaki was thankful for Theodore's very direct advice. She repeated it a few times in her head to make sure she wouldn't forget it. Shuutarou must have been a seasoned player, she surmised based on his human-like summons with miraculous healing skills, his striking armor, and his relaxed attitude.

He's strong, and he has strong summons… I need his help.

She could show him the safest route to the three stranded players, and he would surely be able to help them get out to safety. He seemed like a friendly, good-natured person who wouldn't turn down a request for help. Misaki felt bad about being so calculating, but she was willing to grasp at straws.

"Please—please help me!!"

Tears rolled down her cheeks. She wasn't crying for show to get their sympathy—after her brush with death, she was more emotional than she'd wanted to be.

She told them about the monster horde preparing for an invasion and about how she couldn't join in the battle because she'd been a noncombatant since getting locked in the game. She told them that there weren't enough strong players to guarantee victory against the monsters, that the red mob markers hadn't disappeared yet after two hours since the battle began. That blue dots signifying players were stuck in another part of the tunnel. Once she started talking, she couldn't stop the flood of words.

"I had no idea…," Shuutarou replied when she finished. "Lead the way! We'll do what we can!" he offered cheerfully.

*   *   *   *

The sound of footsteps carried through the tunnel. A small party was coming through. The girl at the front was beaming with hope and determination. A pallid girl and a dark-haired knight walked slightly behind her, with a player in ominous black armor at the rear. Misaki was leading Shuutarou and his summons toward the blue dots on her minimap.

At first, Shuutarou wasn't sure it was a good idea to go with Misaki so far into the tunnel, since she'd had hardly any battle experience, but he agreed in the end, seeing that it was really important to her.

Vampy and Theodore can keep her safe, he reasoned.

In fact, Misaki was safer in the company of Shuutarou's Abyss Slime and the two Evil Overlords than at an inn in Allistras.

"This is the quickest route! I can use my unique skill to warn you of any monsters, so we can avoid encounters," Misaki said, looking at her minimap.

"And which way is the Goblin King?" asked Shuutarou.

"...What?"

Misaki stopped in her tracks.

"I'll remember the location of the stranded players, don't worry. But isn't the squad fighting the Goblin King in even more danger? We should help them, too."

"But the Goblin King is a really high-level mob..."

"We actually came here for the Grand Quest, so we'd be going there anyway!"

Saving the three stranded players was the most Misaki had hoped to achieve. It didn't occur to her that she could ask Shuutarou for help with the goblins as well.

"The Goblin King is around level thirty-five, though! Its mobs are up to level fifteen, and it can raise their stats with its unique skill!"

Misaki couldn't let Shuutarou risk his life without making sure he knew what he was getting himself into.

"A level-thirty-five monster doesn't deserve to call himself a king. He should get to level one hundred twenty like us before making claims to fancy titles," Vampy said, her expression impassive.

"One hundred twenty?!" Misaki couldn't help shouting.

"I should've asked them not to mention their levels..." Shuutarou groaned.

Just like Gallarus, who'd brag about his level at every opportunity, the other Evil Overlords also thought it right and proper to inform everyone about their maxed-out level to indicate their strength and status in the mob hierarchy.

Shuutarou rubbed his forehead, feeling awkward. "Anyway, safe to say we're strong enough. Let's split into two groups at the next branch in the tunnel, if that's okay with you?"

He smiled uncertainly. Not that it could be seen—his helmet covered his face.

With one group going to help the stranded players while another went straight to the Goblin King, they had higher chances of preventing casualties. While Misaki thought about this, Shuutarou spoke to the Evil Overlords via telepathy.

'Mind if one of you guys escorts Misaki here?'

'No need to ask. Your wish is my command, Master,' Vampy replied. Theodore nodded.

The telepathy feature enabled private, mind-to-mind conversation between a master and their subordinates. It was invaluable to Shuutarou, since he could discuss matters related to his dungeon with his minions without the fear of anyone overhearing. The feature was a reward for gaining two demi-human minions and normally took months of skillful dungeon management to unlock.

'Okay! How about Theodore goes with Misaki, and Vampy and I will go to the Goblin King?'

Shuutarou chose Theodore for the escort job because he thought Misaki would feel safer with a grown-up man guarding her.

'Understood.' Theodore accepted the order without protest.

There was actually one more reason Shuutarou thought Theodore was a better choice for keeping Misaki safe—as far as he knew, Theodore was a levelheaded, honorable knight, while Vampy had once tried to kill him with an ax out of curiosity.

After they walked for a while, the tunnel split into two. The right branch led to the goblins, while the left branch led to the stranded players.

"Vampy and I will join the battle. Theodore will go with you, Misaki. Stay safe!"

Shuutarou waved bye and entered the tunnel going right. Vampy bowed quickly and followed him.

"Wait…!"

Shuutarou stopped when Misaki called after him.

She wanted to thank the saintly dark knight, who was in a hurry to help players in need, knowing that every second counted. But the words that came out of her mouth were not what she intended.

"Will I ever see you again?"

She covered her mouth, ashamed—she really shouldn't trouble him anymore, and yet she'd said that.

"Sure!" came his chipper reply.

Shuutarou waved again and walked off into the tunnel.

*　　*　　*　　*

The Crest guild was in dire straits. The Goblin King followed one ferocious attack with another. The attackers were heavily wounded and running low on potions, even though they'd brought loads with them. They owed it to Wataru, who'd been tanking solo for an hour now, that none of the players had died thus far.

"Team Two has lost all their NPCs. Monsters are spawning faster than they can kill them!"

"My weapon's durability's almost at zero! Anyone got a spare one-handed sword?!"

"My leg! My leeeg! Aaargh!"

Flamme surveyed the battlefield, which had turned into a hellscape, with people drenched in blood mixed with sweat and dirt.

People are begging for reinforcements left and right. We don't have any dead yet, but I have a feeling someone's going to die any time now. The plan was to wait for the right moment and wipe all the lesser goblins out at once with third-rank spells, but we're not sufficiently in control of the battle to do that now...

Every single fighter under her command had injuries all over their bodies. One had lost his leg. A healer went to tend to him. But the person closest to death was Wataru. He'd stopped responding to her messages. He was the only player who could kill the Goblin King. If Wataru died, that would spell doom for all of Allistras. It was wiser to retreat and try again later, but Wataru was fighting entirely on autopilot by this point. He wouldn't even fall back when he needed healing. He was in his own world, not part of a team.

"All units, close your ranks and retreat through the Point A pathway! I'll bring up the rear!" Alba shouted out to the desperate troops.

He was still barely standing, using his greatsword like a cane.

"But Wataru's still fighting!" Flamme yelled back frantically.

"We won't go all the way back to the city. I'll block the enemy in that narrow path while you leave the tunnels to regroup outside. Flamme, take all the potions you can get and get to Wataru through the tunnel behind him. My horse can carry both of you to safety."

"O-okay. Got it."

Alba summoned his black horse, which neighed spiritedly as it spawned. Flamme mounted it and clutched the reins.

It would be impossible to reach Wataru on foot with so many enemies around, and attempting to walk by the Goblin King in its current state was suicide. When its LP dropped to 65 percent, its attack pattern changed. The Goblin King switched its weapon from the hatchet to a giant hammer, which struck with a whirlwind effect, causing damage over a wide area. There was now a dead zone around it—one that even goblins wouldn't approach. Wataru was the sole person inside that zone, dodging the hammer again and again, his eyes vacant.

His LP was now at 30 percent.

"What about you, Alba?"

"What about me? No more than four goblins can come at me at once in that narrow pathway. I'll hold out as long as needed and escape once the opportunity presents itself."

Flamme met his eyes, reading in them that he was prepared for death. Fighting back tears, she rode past him, leading her ailing unit out of the tunnels.

Alba stacked Barricade, Steel Defense, and Strengthen skills. After the last of the retreating players passed by him, he cast Provoke on the goblins chasing them and rested his greatsword on his shoulder.

"You shall not pass."

*   *   *   *

Shuutarou and Vampy could see the big cavern now. The players inside were beginning a retreat, but one man was staying behind to stop the goblins from chasing after the others. The player who'd been soloing the Goblin King seemed to already be at his limit.

"Which one of them do we go to first?"

"Master...I have something I must confess."

Shuutarou looked at Vampy, waiting for her to continue.

"I am the Undead Overlord, queen of the highest undead race—the Reapers."

From her tone and expression, Shuutarou could tell she was telling him a great secret that had been weighing heavily on his conscience.

"I cause death wherever I go, simply by the curse of who I am. My unique skill, The End, instantly kills anyone weaker than me within a certain range."

Shuutarou had gone pale under his helmet. Vampy couldn't see that, of course. She continued her painful confession.

"The End also causes anyone I touch, or anyone who touches me, to die within seconds. Even if we are the same level. Can you guess where I'm going with this?"

"How did you get here—?"

"Oh... What are we going to do?! We can't— We can't log out!"

That time he touched her, when they first met...

"The day you arrived in Ross Maora Castle was the first time I had ever been touched by a living being—and yet you did not perish."

Shuutarou reflexively looked at his right hand, remembering another time he and Vampy had physical contact.

"Master, will you be so generous as to indulge my request?"

He thought about the look she gave him then.

"For the first time, I felt the warmth of a human body. On another occasion, I asked you to hold my hand...with the intention of killing you. But you didn't die, and so I didn't meet my end, either."

"Do you feel anything...?"

"Huh? Um...I can feel your hand's smaller than mine!"

"I see..."

Vampy did that in order to die herself. Shuutarou didn't reply. The fact that she had been trying to kill him didn't make him hate her, and it didn't make him afraid anymore as well.

"I didn't want to continue to exist. I wanted to end my realm of chaos and destruction, to kill the other Evil Overlords with their greedy ambitions and contempt for races other than theirs. I've longed to destroy it all, and then you told me that your death would achieve that. That it would kill even me, an undead. That revelation brought me great happiness."

"So I only need to break it—"

"No, no, no, you got it backward! We can't let anyone break it, or we'll all die!"

"So that's why you wanted to hold my hand and destroy the Dungeon Core."

Vampy nodded. "You showed me, cold as ice, what the warmth of the living feels like. You gave the inhabitants of my realm purpose. But as my admiration for you grew, so did the guilt over my past mistakes—mistakes so grave, no apology can ever suffice. I will do anything you ask of me, Master."

Shuutarou's armor melted back into the usual blob shape of Punio. He cuddled the slime in his arms. Vampy could see his face now—he was smiling gently. Her chest tightened with emotion.

Shuutarou raised two fingers.

"Okay, I guess I have two wishes, then! I'd like you to help other players, and to become my friend! Oh, and actually, I have another one, too—please don't try to kill yourself again!"

He quickly raised a third finger.

"Ha-ha, that didn't come out nearly as cool as I'd hoped!"

He'd lifted the terrible weight of Vampy's guilt. She nodded with profound gratitude and headed into the goblin cavern with a spring in her step.

She was going to kill her master's enemies and save his allies. But in order to succeed, she'd have to change her ways—indiscriminate killing wasn't what her master wanted. Never had she imagined that she'd be saving the living. She had to change, and her strong wish to do so refined her unique skill.

Vampy began to dance. She danced like a pure-white angel as countless goblins around her keeled over, crumbling into glittering pixel dust. She danced like a hell-spawned demon, and the ferocious Goblin King dropped to its knees, turning into ashes that fell apart like a burnt piece of paper, disintegrating until nothing was left.

Vampy's The End reached as far as her eyes could see. Anyone she wished dead dissolved into pixels.

Wataru collapsed. The flame of his life was still burning, but only faintly. Around him, lesser goblins perished, the shimmering pixels of their life essence rising into the air in a mesmerizing display before they disappeared.

Vampy turned back toward Shuutarou with a smile. "I have carried out your wishes, Master."

* * * *

A man and a young girl were making their way through the dark tunnels. The man looked up, sensing something.

"Ah, it's over," he said.

"Sorry?"

"See for yourself with your unique skill."

Misaki activated Sense Life, checking her minimap. "Oh! The big red dot is gone!"

The little red dots signifying the regular goblin mobs had also disappeared. One red dot was still there, next to a purple one.

"Shuutarou and Vampy killed the goblins!"

All that remained was for her and Theodore to save the three stranded players. An enormous sense of relief descended on Misaki. It liberated her from the suffocating tightness in her chest, allowing her to breathe easy.

"Vampy's really strong, isn't she? I'm so glad Wataru's team is safe…," she whispered, exhausted.

"…"

Theodore stopped in his tracks. Misaki stopped, too, wondering why he had such a serious look on his face all of a sudden.

"I'd like to ask you not to talk about Vampy to anyone, if possible."

Misaki was surprised, but she thought that was understandable.

"You have your reasons, I suppose," she said with a smile.

"Making a display of power does not befit our master. Dominating others through strength and fear only earns one grudges."

Theodore looked away from Misaki. She could tell that he admired his master.

"I absolutely agree," she told him. "I really admire Wataru, and he doesn't boast about his strength, either. Instead, he offers help and guidance to anyone weaker than him."

Misaki glanced at Theodore, thinking about how thankful she was to Shuutarou for agreeing to help her with her self-imposed mission, and how he'd saved Wataru and all the players who came to fight the goblins, as well as the entire city of Allistras. She promised herself she'd repay him for that.

"I promise not to talk about Shuutarou, you, or Vampy. The last thing I want is to cause you trouble after all you've done for me."

"I appreciate that."

Theodore looked into Misaki's eyes and found in them sincerity and honor. Pleased, he opened his inventory and retrieved a few items.

"This isn't a bribe for keeping quiet about us, but I happen to have some pieces of equipment I made for Master, which he no longer needs. If you can put them to good use, I'd rather you have them."

He handed the bewildered girl an astonishingly lightweight yet extremely durable bow made from multilayered silver and a quiver of silver arrows. Theodore had gotten a bit carried away and made the bow and arrows along with every single weapon and armor type he knew for Shuutarou to browse back when he invited the boy to his realm.

The metal bow was even lighter than Misaki's wooden Beginner's Bow. She weighed it in her hands, getting a feel for it.

"This bow…"

"It's nothing special. I make things like that in my spare time."

Misaki pulled the bowstring back a few times. Her eyes widened in surprise.

"It's so easy to draw! And it weighs hardly anything, but the tension is excellent!"

"I tried to pick the best alloys for it. It should serve you better than that piece of wood."

"Are you sure you want me to have it?"

"I am. Take this, too, for close-range combat. To excel at any range, you might want to learn close-quarter combat skills."

He handed her a dagger. Similarly to Shuutarou's sword, it had a very basic design. The blade was see-through thin, and featherlight.

Misaki equipped the weapons—the Silver Bow, Silver Arrows, and Fang Dagger—and immediately felt braver, more protected.

"And a little charm for you."

Theodore was enveloped in a dark aura. He put one hand on Misaki's head, and the aura appeared around her as well. She looked at her hands curiously.

Theodore crossed his arms. "I gave you two buffs: Life Link, so that we may share LP, and Dragon Lord's Blessing, to boost your stats. When the dark aura disappears, it means they've worn off."

Misaki could sense that her body was stronger—her brain was registering her digital body as her real body, so the buffs had an instant, palpable effect.

Theodore had done what he could for her. He resumed walking toward the players they were to rescue.

"Why are you going out of your way to help me?" Misaki asked, confused.

"Master ordered me to protect you. I do my utmost to carry out his orders to the letter," Theodore replied matter-of-factly. He stopped without turning back to look at her. "You will need the buffs and the equipment I gave you if you want to continue going this way."

"But…what exactly is up ahead?"

Theodore was already walking off. He didn't clarify what he meant. Misaki hurried after him so as not to be left behind.

* * * *

Three shadows separated from the darkness of the tunnel. Lanterns swayed as they walked by, treading on purple flowers growing on the cave floor.

The player killer Black Dog kicked a pebble irritably.

"Why the hell's no one coming after us?" he asked his companion.

"Because they're too busy with the Goblin King? They may all end up dead if you keep hanging around here."

Kijima, another player killer, chortled at that. "Our plan went up in smoke because you overlooked the radar girl. Rookie mistake. The three of us would've been able to kill Alba easily."

The shadowy figure in the middle drew his sword. Flames flickered across the blade, illuminating the wielder's face—it was Kidd.

"What difference does it make? You want everyone dead, you'll get everyone dead. I reported all noteworthy unique skills to you. The invasion's going to crush the city. What do you have to complain about?"

Black Dog and Kijima knew about the monster group in the tunnels before anyone else because that's where they lived, unable to enter cities with their negative karma. They'd been killing players who ventured into the tunnels since the day they'd all become trapped in the game. They'd been stockpiling items and equipment looted from their victims, awaiting the day of the invasion with anticipation. In the past, during beta, when invading monsters destroyed the town gates, the system block that prevented player killing within the town became disabled. Kijima and Black Dog were planning on taking advantage of the invasion to enter Allistras, where they'd take the lives of the three hundred fifty thousand players who'd been sheltering inside, scared for their lives. They'd gotten addicted to the twisted pleasure of killing people for real. They hadn't killed everyone they met, though—they recruited one person as an ally. That was Kidd.

"I guess it works for us either way."

"As long as I get to feast on both Crest and the tender civilians, it's fine by me."

The two whimsical murderers chuckled. Kidd scratched his head to distract himself from feeling annoyed by them. They had scouted him in Ilyana Tunnel. After that, he joined Crest to spy for them.

"Hey, I have a deal you can't refuse. Well, you can refuse, but then you die," Black Dog had whispered into Kidd's ear after rendering him immobile that time when he attacked Kidd's party. Black Dog activated his unique skill, Death's Promise, on Kidd, who was in critical condition.

Death's Promise postponed imminent death for another player, force-adding them to the skill user's party. Leaving the party would kill that player at once. When *Eternity* was just a game, it was a weird but worthless skill—players would just leave the party, die, and respawn. But with real death as the penalty for leaving Black Dog's party, Kidd had no choice but to do his bidding. He failed to lure Alba into the tunnels when Hunting Party Seventeen got wiped out, but he supplied the killers with valuable information about the Crest members' unique skills, and it didn't take him too long to catch wind of Misaki, which allowed the killers to come up with a new plan for the invasion day.

Black Dog attacked Alba, and Kidd chased after him, pretending to be blinded by rage. Crest had been barely winning against the Goblin King, and with the loss of two key people, they found themselves in a desperate situation.

If the players managed to kill the Goblin King somehow, the killers would ambush them before they had time to heal up after that ordeal. If they all died, the monsters would storm Allistras, breaking the city gates and letting the player killers in to wreak havoc inside. Either scenario was fine from their point of view.

Kijima cracked his neck.

"Enough waiting around. Let's go have some fun."

Black Dog drew his dagger, excitement making him impatient. They started walking toward Crest's main unit, through a network of tunnels that would take them right behind the fighters.

"..."

Past conversations with the Crest members he'd been teaching to fight replayed in Kidd's mind.

"Could you help me with my skill tree, Kidd?"

"Is this the right weapon for me?"

"Can we practice together?"

"I'm sorry I was an ass to you earlier..."

He'd been acting friendly toward them only to learn what their unique skills were. He didn't want them to die, but it was too late. He couldn't pull out of this, not after he'd aided the killers in injuring Alba. He was already a traitor.

"Hope that chick who's tight with Wataru and Alba is still alive."

"Why? You got the hots for her or something?"

"Hey, I like my women strong. Isn't it so cute when they put on a brave face right until the end?"

The player killers' nasty laughter echoed off the walls. They were strong and cruel. They reckoned that if they got to kill Crest's top people, they'd gain power unmatched by any other player in the game.

Kidd was remembering his friends, now dead.

"You're so lucky, Kidd! Only a hundred players will get to play the beta, and you're one of them!"

"We'll catch up to you when the game opens for everyone!"

"If you're gonna be the damage dealer, I'll play a tank. He can be a healer."

"Lend me that flame sword one day!"

"I don't feel so scared about being trapped in the game with you guys here."

"If one of us dies, it's on the survivors to notify their parents about what happened, okay?"

Kidd stopped walking. The player killers didn't notice.

This may be my only chance. If I act fast...

He left their party.

Black Dog's some upper-rank thief class. His skills mostly rely on catching the target unawares. His unique skill is irrelevant at the moment. Kijima's a caster and has no close-range abilities. He forgot to cast a barrier spell...

Watching his LP rapidly drain away, Kidd activated Body Flicker to snap to his targets instantly, followed up by Draw Sword, Fierce Strike, and Quick-Draw Slash with his fiery blade. Two heads rolled down onto the ground. Kidd felt the effort of the swift combo in his muscles.

"Told you to give it up, didn't I?" came a voice from behind.

The headless bodies crumpled onto the ground and disappeared like fading mirages. A powerful blow pushed Kidd against a wall. He glared hatefully at the two player killers over his shoulder.

"Thought you might try to betray us, so I had my skill active. Your timing couldn't have been better," Kijima said, roaring with laughter.

Kidd followed Kijima's gaze to a patch of purple flowers under a lantern. Their petals were dropping off as the flowers withered. Kidd cursed himself for his lack for foresight.

I've been teaching rookies to watch out for their opponents' unique skills, but I failed to take that into account myself... Pathetic.

His life was about to be extinguished. He didn't struggle—it was a tranquil process.

"I like that my skill doesn't cause instant death; that'd rob me of the pleasure of seeing this delicious hopelessness in your eyes."

Black Dog leaned his face closer.

"You're gross!" Kijima tutted at him.

I didn't want the face of my friends' murderer to be the last thing I see before dying...

Kidd shut his eyes, teetering on the brink of consciousness.

Suddenly, there was a change in the air. Surprised, Kijima turned toward where the tunnel opened onto the goblin cavern.

"The Goblin King's dead...?"

The battle seemed to be over. The other goblins were quickly disappearing.

"That was over in a flash. Weird. Anyhow, Crest must be on its last legs. Shall we?"

Black Dog shot one last look at Kidd, who was pinned to the wall, his feet beginning to dissolve into pixel shards.

"Yeah. I've had enough of toying with this guy."

"Don't you feel sorry for him? If any of his guild members survive to tell the story, he'll go down as a traitor," Kijima said mockingly.

Kidd had no strength left to say anything back. He vacantly stared at his unraveling body.

I failed...everyone...

A single tear rolled down his cheek.

"There they are!" someone shouted happily.

The player killers spun around toward the voice. A girl with shaggy brown hair and beginners' equipment was waving at them. Kijima and Black Dog exchanged glances, exhaling loudly as they lowered their guard.

"What are you doing here?"

"Got lost? Or were you looking for somebody?"

They slowly approached her, and only then, they noticed a black-haired man in armor standing nearby. They became wary again.

"Are you from Crest?" Kijima asked with menace in his voice.

"Um, no, I'm not with them. I came here by myself to save you!"

Kijima and Black Dog smirked with amusement. She'd be an appetizer before the feast they were going to have soon after.

Shuutarou took care of the dangerous goblins, but I have to finish what I came here for!

Misaki was relieved to see that the two players, who'd come out of the shadows to where a lantern was casting faint light, seemed to be unhurt. They had almost stumbled into the cavern where the battle was taking place!

"Run! They're player killers!" Kidd shouted hoarsely with the last ounce of his strength.

Misaki gasped when she noticed him pinned to the wall. The next moment, his body shattered into pixels.

Did he just…die?

She could see the other players' faces now in the light. Her body tensed with fear.

"So nice to meet you, young lady. What level are you?"

"Killing chicks is special. I love it."

The man in tattered gray robes and another, his face half hidden by the hood of his cape, smiled at her nastily. They had been among the hundred lucky players to gain access during the beta. They hunted players on field maps, killing so many that they became banned from towns and cities. Kijima and Black Dog were serial killers.

Black Dog motioned with his head toward where Kidd had died, leaving behind a pile of items. He sighed. "Pity it's just you and no Crest members coming along to see us. That dude had no talent for luring in prey."

Misaki was confused. *Who are these people? They were talking about killing Crest members a moment earlier. They're not some scared players who got lost in the tunnels.*

Kijima laughed at Misaki, who remained clueless. "You came here to save us, huh? How precious, how brave! How *suicidal*! You really are dumb, you know?"

"You can't seriously be plotting to kill people who are doing everything to help everyone! We're not just data; we're real people!" Misaki shouted, her voice quavering.

Kijima shrugged.

"I like to keep it simple. If you're strong, you can do whatever you like. There are no laws here. Eat, fuck, kill, steal—those are the things I wanna do, and no one can stop me. I love this world, and I don't want anybody 'freeing us' from it."

The echo repeated his laughter again and again. Misaki bit her lip bloody, tears streaming down her cheeks.

I'm so stupid… I thought they got stuck here and needed help. It never crossed my mind they might be bad people…

Kijima and Black Dog moved in unison to attack her. Misaki clutched her dagger defensively, but her fear was so disabling that she couldn't move, staring in terror as the killers stabbed her back, chest, throat. She was going to die…

A number flashed in her UI every time the killers attacked.

85,921,506,797
85,921,506,797
85,921,506,797

She realized what it was.

"What the hell…? How strong is this girl?!"

"Is she one of the frontline players?! No, no way—even then, she wouldn't be so high level that none of my attacks would deal damage!"

They didn't leave a scratch on her, a fact that made them scared.

The number was Misaki's LP, increased by half of Theodore's plus an extra amount from having her stats boosted by Dragon Lord's Blessing to values normally reached by level-80 players. Not to mention she was wearing exceptional equipment. Since it was originally intended for Shuutarou, each item was a masterpiece, with stat boosts.

Resistance to damage was based on relevant numerical values. If your defense was high enough, someone could strike you with a blade, and it would bounce right off your bare skin.

The player killers backed away, wary of a counterattack.

"Uh… *Huff…*"

Misaki collapsed, eyes wide-open, heart racing to the point where it hurt. She felt so useless after being completely unable to react to the attacks, aware that they would've killed her if it hadn't been for

Theodore. She pressed her hand to her chest, bending down. At least she hadn't dropped her dagger.

"Enough." A voice broke the silence.

The player killers felt blood drain out of their faces as Theodore approached, sliding his sinister-looking sword out of its scabbard. Practiced killers, they could sense when someone was a greater threat. They felt something unavoidable was coming.

Theodore swung his greatsword at the pair.

"No, wai—"

The sword cut straight through them, and they burst into a scattering of pixels. In less than a second, they were dead. Misaki witnessed their deaths right in front of her eyes.

She was crying again—she'd lost track of how many times she'd cried that day. She looked up at Theodore, her eyes glazed over.

"I apologize," he told her. "I was aware that the players you had been seeking were evildoers. I'm sorry I did not warn you."

Theodore sheathed his sword. The words got stuck in Misaki's throat, so she just shook her head frantically.

He'd given her great weapons, and yet she couldn't do anything. In the end, he had to dirty his hands saving her.

He came with me knowing all along that I was leading him to those murderers. He anticipated that I'd need his help, that fear would root me to the spot...

What if it hadn't been Theodore who'd come along with her, but a player she'd managed to recruit at an inn? Or kind Flamme, who hugged her when she cried? Or Alba, or Wataru? Her ignorance and obsessive sense of duty might have gotten them killed.

Realizing that, Misaki was overwhelmed with gratitude for Theodore. It was thanks to him that she'd lived to learn from her mistake.

Misaki looked over at the piles of items left behind where the three players had died. Without saying a word, she picked up the items and put them in her storage.

Until Misaki stood up from the ground on her own, Theodore had been silently standing beside her.

*   *   *   *

A little earlier...

Alba swung his greatsword, which had been on the verge of breaking, at the green foes that kept coming at him endlessly. He avoided glancing at his LP bar, which was diminishing bit by bit, withstanding the attacks in order to give his allies time to safely retreat.

Flamme should have reached the retreat point by now. Maybe she's already retrieved Wataru and is riding back with him...

Alba nearly lost his balance. He steadied himself, grasping the blood-soaked hilt of his sword more firmly. Like a god of war, he summoned the last of his strength, pushing back the horde of goblins. If he managed to draw the attention of the goblin boss to himself, his job would be done.

They'll have to be quick in finding someone to fill my shoes if they're to keep danger at bay. A tall order, that one.

He laughed inwardly. It was all in the hands of the younger players now. He knew he wouldn't make it out alive. He hoped that his sacrifice would enable the surviving players to come up with a better strategy based on what they'd learned from this battle and stop the monsters before they invaded the city. It amused him to think that he was taking the easy way out dying here, leaving all those problems for the others to solve.

His LP had dropped below 20 percent, and he really was on his last legs.

Alba noticed something unexpected.

Seems like there's fewer goblins around...

The ceaseless stream of enemies coming his way had dwindled to a trickle. Fewer and fewer goblins were showing up until there were no more. The silence, after so many hours of fighting, had an unnatural quality to it. Dragging his feet on the floor, which was slippery from blood, Alba made his way down toward the goblin cavern.

Am I dreaming? What could've happened?

The cavern was empty. Only the ruins of their temporary settlement were left behind, damaged in battle, with an empty throne in their midst.

"Alba!"

"Flamme! And Wataru… Thank goodness!"

Flamme appeared, looking as confused as Alba. She was on his black horse, with Wataru lying unconscious across the horse's back like a sack. Green liquid was dripping from his hair. Maybe Flamme had doused him with recovery potions instead of having him drink them.

Alba and Flamme warily surveyed what remained of the goblin's settlement.

"This isn't your doing, is it?" he asked her.

"As if! The Goblin King's dead, too. Wataru's strongest magic was hitting it only for a few percent of its LP, but all of a sudden, it's dead."

Alba nodded slowly, wondering whether it was possible that the goblins hadn't been defeated but disappeared on their own.

"Maybe there was a time limit to this event, and they despawned because we took so long?"

"No, Alba. We wouldn't have gotten EXP from them if that was the case, and we did get loads."

Alba opened his menu and saw that his level had gone up from 37 to 40. The game featured quests with time limits, but no one had ever received a reward from a quest where monsters disappeared due to naturally timing out. The EXP from the goblin mobs Alba had killed wouldn't be sufficient to earn him three levels. No—someone had defeated the Goblin King, completing the quest, and they seemingly accomplished that in an instant. Everyone who participated in the battle received a share of EXP and loot. But who did that? And when did they join the battle? Where had their savior disappeared off to?

"Anyway, let's get out of here, Alba. Everyone's waiting outside."

"Yes, let's. But I wouldn't mind if you gave me some recovery potions first."

Flamme picked out the strongest one she had and handed it to Alba. He pulled the cork out of the bottle…and poured the liquid on his head. The cold sensation, strong grassy smell, and green droplets getting in his eyes confirmed to him that this was reality.

"Why'd you do that?"

"I thought maybe I was dreaming, and I'd wake up in a hospital bed. I might've preferred that, actually…"

"Ha-ha. It's no dream, just virtual reality!"

It felt good to be able to joke again.

They headed out of the tunnels, staying cautious just in case. Outside, they were greeted by all the other players who'd participated in the battle, who cheered with happy tears in their eyes, lining up to hug them.

* * * *

The fighters returned to Allistras, and the empty streets rapidly filled with people commending the heroes. Alba walked down the main street among falling cherry blossoms. NPCs were out, rejoicing that the danger of invasion had been averted, and even the timid players who'd been holed up at the inns the whole time opened their windows to wave. The scenery and NPC behavior were part of a scripted event for when players managed to prevent an invasion that would otherwise have destroyed the city. Even the ex–beta testers hadn't experienced it before.

"Where am I…?"

"Wataru! You finally woke up!"

Flamme's voice quavered as she swallowed back tears of joy. Still on horseback, Wataru sat up, looking dazed, not understanding how he'd gotten out of the dark tunnel with swarms of goblins to the busy city with people clapping all around.

"Is this a dream?"

Alba hoisted him onto his shoulder from the horse and put him on the ground. That woke up Wataru properly. He looked around at the crowds, at the petals dancing in the air, at the white doves flying triumphantly toward the sky as music filled the streets. It was as if this joyous festival had been prepared in advance, with the city confident in the players' victory—but of course, it'd just been instantly generated by the game's engine the moment the grand quest had been completed.

"It may take you a while to wrap your head around what happened, but know that it's over—we won."

Wataru finally smiled. He gazed up at the blue sky awash with relief, his efforts rewarded.

*   *   *   *

Shuutarou and Vampy were in the woods not too far from the Ilyana Tunnel entrance. Misaki spotted them and came running, beaming happily.

"Shuutarou!"

"Glad to see you're okay, Misaki!"

"M-me too… Thank goodness…you're all right…"

She had to pause to wipe her tears, which were flowing too easily now, after that dramatic day. Then she bowed her head to Vampy.

"Thank you so much for your help as well. Because of you, the Crest guild safely returned to the city, and there were no casualties."

Misaki knew that from her minimap. Sense Life showed her Shuutarou's location and the players reaching Allistras. She counted them—there was one fewer blue dot than at the start of the battle, and eight fewer green dots. The green ones were NPCs, and the missing blue dot was Kidd.

"I see," Vampy replied curtly.

Misaki wondered why Vampy seemed to be in a bad mood.

"Good to have you back, Theodore! Seems I made the right call sending you in there with Misaki."

"I fulfilled your orders to the best of my ability, Master."

Theodore had been in telepathic contact with Shuutarou the entire time, so the boy knew about the player killers and about Theodore having given Misaki weapons. He'd been worried when Theodore told him about the girl suffering shock from witnessing the deaths of other players, but to his great relief, Misaki seemed to have recovered her determination and strong will.

They chatted for a while before Shuutarou decided it was time to go back.

"I'd love to see the city now that everything's fine again, but I don't want to startle people, so I'm gonna head home for now."

"You're not coming?"

Shuutarou looked pointedly down at his ominous black armor. The corners of Misaki's lips turned downward in disappointment, but she didn't feel it was right for her to insist.

"...Then I'll go back to Allistras! I want to check on everyone at the guild anyway," Misaki said.

"Okay, cool. But it's a bit of a hike, and there's monsters on the way there, so let me walk you to the city gates!"

"No, you don't have to! Theodore gave me these wonderful weapons. I can make it back on my own—don't worry!"

He really was so nice, it made Misaki even sadder to part ways with him, but she did her best not to show it.

"All right, then!"

The two Evil Overlords flanked him, and Shuutarou moved his hand, opening his menu. Misaki could tell he was getting ready to depart somewhere.

"Thank you for everything, Theodore! I'll treasure the weapons you gave me and your words of wisdom! I learned so much from you."

Misaki bowed to Theodore resolutely. He folded his arms and smiled at her.

"Keep up your training, then."

She nodded several times. She would work tirelessly at improving her battle abilities, so as not to waste the precious weapons he'd gifted her. Theodore nodded back to her, approving of her spirit.

"Okay, Misaki, we'll be going now! See you again sometime!"

Shuutarou waved. Misaki pressed her lips into a smile. A moment later, he and his two companions were gone in a flash of bright light, which lingered briefly. The forest was silent except for the singing of birds. Misaki stared for a while at this glowing afterimage before turning to walk to the city.

* * * *

Squeezing through crowds of people celebrating the triumphant return of the fighters, Misaki wove her way to the Adventurers Guild.

Whoa, it's packed here, too...

The guild house was bursting with NPCs and players in gray armor. No sooner had Misaki entered than she heard someone shout her name.

"Misaki!"

"Oh, Flam—"

Flamme rushed to Misaki, hugging her with such force that she pushed her onto the ground. She rubbed her cheek against Misaki's.

"I'm so happy you're okay, Flamme!"

"Safe and sound!" Flamme saluted playfully.

She had already messaged Misaki to let her know everything was well, and she knew that Misaki had been checking in on her using Sense Life, but that didn't detract from their joyful reunion.

"I've never seen it so busy here," said Misaki.

"It's mostly NPCs, though. Looks like a special event for thwarting a large-scale monster invasion."

Everywhere was packed, making for a stark difference from when the city had been locked down.

A stately man of impressive physique and a younger man with handsome features and faded brown hair made their way to Flamme and Misaki.

Misaki was enormously relieved. The invasion didn't happen, and everything was all right.

"You're unhurt! Both of you!"

"Can't believe it myself," Wataru said with a laugh.

He made it sound like a joke, but it was the truth. Toward the end of the battle, both he and Alba had been fighting out of sheer stubbornness, prepared for death. Wataru was flicking in and out of consciousness as he tanked the Goblin King without help, while Alba blocked the goblin horde from chasing after the retreating players. Thinking back, Alba was terrified by his own daredevil attitude, but for Wataru, who had passed out in the end, it hadn't even sunken in just how close to death he'd been.

They chatted pleasantly, happy to see each other. Wataru turned to Misaki with an eager expression on his face.

"Would you like to join our guild, Misaki?"

Being invited directly by the guild master was a huge honor, Misaki felt. She hadn't given much thought to her future in the game—her head had been too full of worries about the goblins. She thought for a moment, but it wasn't much of a dilemma.

"Yes, I'd love to!"

"Yaaaay! Awesome!!"

Flamme pushed her over again with another energetic hug. Wataru and Alba prepared the official invite right away. Misaki skimmed over the guild agreement they sent her, then pressed JOIN while still in Flamme's crushing embrace. The name tags of Wataru, Flamme, and Alba changed from white to blue for her as she became their guildmate.

Her face suddenly clouded with worry. "But...won't it upset some people that I joined without proving that I'm capable?"

She remembered the guild members at the inn who shouted abuse at her when she implored them to go with her to Ilyana Tunnel. Now that she was in Crest, she was bound to see them every now and again, and being in the same group with people who were openly hostile toward her would be bad for her mental health.

"Don't worry about that," Alba said to her. "We have you to thank for discovering the goblin colony. Be proud, because you helped to prevent the invasion."

Seeing things this way cheered her up. If anyone in the guild harbored ill feelings toward her, she'd try to clear things up with them when it came to it. It was okay for her to be happy about the guild invitation. She smiled.

Glad to have her on board, Wataru busied himself with his menu. His guild hadn't yet claimed the reward for completing the goblin Grand Quest since he, Alba, and Flamme had prioritized getting Misaki to join before taking care of other business. Her unique skill really was priceless to them.

The moment he claimed the reward, the Adventurers Guild NPCs who'd been excitedly celebrating the city being saved calmed down at once and began to return to their usual posts. The front-desk NPC made a little speech.

"Thank you to all the brave adventurers who saved the city of Allistras from the threat of monster invasion. Please accept a reward from the Guild first."

All players in the building lit up with glowing auras signifying that they'd leveled up. The NPC went on to list the monsters slain in the quest:

119 goblins
36 Goblin Mages
33 Goblin Soldiers
3 Goblin Thieves
1 Goblin King

Players received EXP, gold, and items in addition to the EXP from killing the monsters. It was a very generous reward. Wataru leveled up from level 42 to 45, Alba to 43, and Flamme to 40. Other participants also gained at least a few levels.

"I'm up three whole levels?"

"Our guild just got a lot stronger."

Wataru and Alba exchanged surprised looks.

Misaki got to level 27. She'd also leveled up earlier when Theodore killed the player killers. She smiled somewhat bitterly, thinking that it was ironic she got so many levels but still had hardly any battle experience.

Every player who took part in the quest received 480,000G. Considering that they barely escaped with their lives, it wasn't that much, but it would allow them to live comfortably in the city.

Everyone also received five different pieces of equipment. Flamme sighed, looking at a chunky one-handed sword that'd materialized in her hand. "It would've been more help if they'd given us all that before we went off to fight the goblins."

"That's how it is in games, Flamme...," Misaki reasoned with her grumpy friend.

They heard a lot of happy voices around as everyone seemed satisfied with the amount. Never mind that their lives were worth much more. They had fought fiercely to save their city and received a grand reward, reaffirming their conviction that they'd done the right thing.

The front-desk NPC went back to their usual work, and a richly dressed elderly NPC stepped forward to talk to the players. Not even the ex–beta testers had ever seen this NPC before, but everyone realized this was a very important character, and they stopped to listen to what he'd have to say.

"The city of Allistras would like to present you with a reward separate from what you've received from the Adventurers Guild."

This was a first—ever since the beta, never had a quest giver offered players an extra reward on top of what they got from the guild, even when the quest was about preventing an invasion. Flamme wondered if this was a special event triggered only by the largest invasions.

"Our saviors who are unaffiliated with a guild shall all receive three hundred fifty thousand gold and the Hero of Allistras title. For the Crest guild, which valiantly led the effort to stop the monster invasion that would have obliterated our city, I have a special reward—henceforth, Allistras is Crest's territory," the elder announced in a grand voice.

When set in the status menu, the Hero of Allistras title changed the behavior of Allistras NPCs toward the player to the friendliest variant. This unlocked special quests, lowered the prices of items in stores, and allowed players to sell items to NPCs for more gold than usual. The effect was limited to this one city, but this was currently the hometown for nearly all of them. With this title, the money they received from the grand quest would go even further, so that they could enjoy a more carefree life for a while.

The unaffiliated players set this new title at once. It appeared above their name tags.

"We don't get the hero title?"

"How come the guildless players get a better reward than us?"

The Crest members thought they were being treated unfairly. Meanwhile, Wataru received a message explaining what it meant to hold territory.

"Everyone, listen up. I just received the following message. I'm going to read it aloud."

The players around him perked up their ears.

"'When a town or city becomes the territory of a guild, the guild becomes able to charge a tax in return for ensuring the territory's safety. The guild may use their territory's defense armaments as they see fit.'"

About half of the players nodded, as that made sense to them, while the other half cocked their heads, not sure what the benefit to them really was. Flamme clarified the message:

"Basically, our guild will be periodically receiving funds from the city! And we've been designated the official peacekeepers of Allistras!"

Again, only about half of the players rejoiced at the news, but Flamme chose not to pay them any mind.

"It's that second part that's the big one," she whispered in Wataru's ear.

"Yes, that stood out to me immediately. This is more than I had hoped for..."

Wataru was really excited, to no one's surprise.

There were three kinds of defensive armaments in Allistras:

magical artillery, magical defense walls, and magical barriers. Guild members would be able to activate them at the cost of gold and some magic. The magical barrier in particular would be invaluable to Crest.

"A magical barrier can hide the city from mobs. Each activation lasts for up to a week. We'd have no more need for patrols and night watches."

"This is huge..."

With this, they could guarantee everyone's safety within the city walls while also freeing up the guild's top players to leave the city and join the front line if they wished.

* * * *

A large, fortified building appeared in Allistras, with white walls and a blue roof. This was the new Crest HQ.

"Staff NPCs, battle training will be your top priority!" Flamme ordered, and the NPCs headed over to the training grounds.

They were new NPCs who came with the guild HQ to help with any odd jobs. There were a hundred of them. They took orders from players with guild-leader privileges and were actually pretty useful. Looking back at how the soldier NPCs got easily wiped out by the goblins, Flamme selected eighty of their personal guild NPCs to become warriors and saw to it that they trained to become stronger. High-level NPCs should be able to protect the noncombatants to some extent.

"It's going to get busy," Wataru said with a smile.

"Indeed. We're finally moving forward with our plans," replied Alba. "By the way, Wataru...I managed to confirm that Kidd's name had turned black."

"Ah... His thirst for revenge was his own undoing in the end. There might've been more than one player killer lying in wait...and they may still be lurking in Ilyana Tunnel."

Wataru and Alba were greatly saddened by Kidd's death. They didn't know that he was a traitor.

Misaki overheard what they were talking about and piped up:

"I was there when he died!"

Wataru and Alba turned to her in surprise. Misaki explained how she'd mistaken the killers for players in distress and gone to help them. Of course, she didn't mention her encounter with Shuutarou and his mobs, making it sound as if she'd been alone the whole time.

She took out a sword from her storage to show them and also displayed some items she picked up from the loot piles left by the player killers.

Wataru opened his eyes wide. "I recognize this…"

"When I got to those players' location, they were already dead," Misaki told him, hanging her head. "These items were left behind, on top of many more…"

Wataru and Alba solemnly took the items from her. Wataru held Kidd's sword reverently. "It seems you've had your revenge, eliminating the other threat in the tunnels. Thank you."

The door to the guild HQ opened, and a crowd of people came in. They were all noncombatants.

Alba frowned. "What's this about…?"

He had a bad feeling, only too aware of the selfish attitudes the noncombatants had displayed in the run-up to the goblin battle, but everyone in the crowd seemed contrite, if anything. Misaki spotted one of the men who'd shouted at her when she tried to recruit help. He gathered up his courage and stepped forward.

"We've come to thank you in person for risking your lives to protect the city. We've also come to apologize for our cowardice, for hiding from any responsibility. Thank you, and sorry."

He bowed his head low, and others followed suit. A few hundred people were making a sincere apology to Crest.

Alba shot Wataru a look. Wataru nodded.

"We're not that much stronger than you, nor much more courageous. One of us lost his life in that battle, but we wouldn't have won if it weren't for his contribution."

The noncombatants listened with rapt attention, and even Crest members fell silent to capture Wataru's every word.

"We gained more, besides preventing this monster invasion. The reward far exceeded my hopes. I can promise you now that even if another invasion were to happen, the city would be absolutely safe for a minimum of seven days."

The crowd didn't come to see him to ask about the battle results, but Wataru told them about the gains to give these poor people a sense of safety they'd so desperately missed. Freed from the fetters of terror, they reacted with great excitement, hugging one another, bursting into tears, and cheering loudly.

"You saved us, and we'd like to repay you any way we can. We'll fight, and we'll travel far on missions if needed," the man who spoke earlier, representing the group, said with tears streaming down his cheeks. "We'll do everything we can to help free all players from this game as soon as possible."

Smiling as before, Wataru reached to shake his hand. One thousand and eighty-eight players joined Crest that day.

"All combatants, please come this way to the training grounds…"

"Excellent. We've had a shortage of crafters…"

"Here's what you do for monster-slaying quests…"

"Urgh. At this rate, I'll be making guild uniforms until the server shuts down…"

The Crest HQ became a hive of activity. Misaki watched for a while before quietly slipping outside, where she lifted her head to gaze at the clear sky.

"Thank you…"

She was immensely grateful to Shuutarou and his mob friends for achieving peace in Allistras. Crest had prevented the monsters' advance on the city, but it was Shuutarou, Vampy, and Theodore who'd taken care of the greatest threats—the Goblin King and the player killers.

Misaki stroked the hilt of her dagger. She made a promise in her heart to be brave and rise to any challenge that might await, getting stronger so that one day she'd be able to repay them for all they'd done for her.

* * * *

Meanwhile, at Ross Maora Castle...

"Master! Take me with you next time you go out!"

"No one said we'd be taking turns. I will accompany Master on his next outing as well."

Bertrand and Vampy glared at each other. Shuutarou was sitting on the throne, kicking his legs, only half listening to the quarreling Evil Overlords.

I hope Misaki made it back okay...

He stroked Punio, which undulated gently, enjoying the affection.

...

...

...

...

The players escaped the worst-case scenario of being wiped out in the starting city. Wataru's guild, Crest, had fought valiantly, securing peace for Allistras. They could now move on to making preparations for traveling to the farthest outposts that'd been reached by players since the beginning of the game.

Changed by her encounter with Theodore, Misaki resolved to make every effort to help find a way out of the prison of the game and back to the real world.

Shuutarou had become the master of Evil Overlords, mysterious mobs whose roles in the game remained unclear. Were they friends...or enemies?

Whom had the Mother AI told the players to defeat?

What were the conditions for clearing the game?

End of Volume 1

Lendos, which meant *water paradise* in the older variant of the Armeldas language, was a peaceful country famous for its natural scenery and countless lakes. One day, a spellbindingly beautiful baby was born in this country. Her name was Lou Vampia Cilrulis, and she was a princess.

The girl, with snow-white skin and near-translucent white hair, was much loved by her royal parents, who did what they could to ensure she had a happy childhood. She'd frequently be seen playing with commoner children, who liked her energy and cheerful nature.

But then her tenth birthday came. This was an important occasion for children both of high and common birth, marking their passage from childhood to adulthood with the revelation of their unique skill. In other countries, children blessed with powerful unique skills would normally be sent to military academies so that they might become soldiers. This wasn't the case in Lendos, which did not wage wars on other lands, nor was it ever a target for attack, owing to its abundance of natural resources paired with excellent foreign relations. Lendos children were free to choose their own future... At least, that was the assumption.

* * * *

Vampia, her common-born friend Leo, and many other girls and boys gathered at the temple where the unique-skill announcement ceremony was to be held.

"I'll get a strong skill and become your personal guard, Vampia!" Leo said.

"What would I do with someone as troublesome as you protecting me? Thanks, but no."

"Sheesh! Anyway, no matter what unique skills we get, we're friends forever, right?"

They fist-bumped, smiling at each other. They came up with fist-bumping as their special sign of friendship and thought it was pretty cool.

Vampia's gaze swept through the crowd. She noticed her father, the king, on the upper floor of the temple looking down at the children gathered below. She smiled and waved.

"Come forward when your name is called," an old priest began, and the children stopped chattering.

The priest called the children one by one. He'd take their hand in his and, with a flash of soft light, produce a square sheet of paper out of his breast pocket. The knight general who accompanied him would take that piece of paper, which detailed the child's unique skill, and read it out to general applause.

"Crop Production Increase, Talking to Animals, Smithing Boost... We're seeing many wonderful skills this year," the priest remarked to the knight general with a friendly smile.

"Ha-ha! Yes, wonderful skills for peaceful times. That's great, as far as I'm concerned," the knight general replied good-naturedly.

The priest called the next child:

"Lou Vampia Cilrulis!"

The white-haired princess made her way to the priest.

"Feeling tense?" the knight general asked.

She shook her head, smiling. "Not one bit! I'm really excited!"

"Oh-ho-ho! That's the spirit, Princess!"

The priest nodded a few times and took her hand.

In an instant, all the 138 children around them fell over.

"What...?"

The children were dead, their corpses lying in a circle around the petrified Vampia, the priest, and the general.

The priest reached into his pocket with a shaking hand, took out a piece of paper, and passed it to the general. No sooner had he done that than he crumpled onto the ground himself, breaking up into shiny shards that quickly disappeared, leaving behind a pile of items.

"No!!!" the general shouted piercingly.

He looked at the piece of paper, reading it quickly...and screamed.

The End: Instantly kills everyone weaker than self within a certain area. Kills targets of lower or similar strength with a touch.

The princess had shot up from level 10 to level 31. A monster was born—a monster who would decide the fate of her country.

The people who had been standing behind the children began fleeing. Vampia turned and saw that all her friends were gone.

"Leo? Why is everyone…?" Her fearful voice broke, tears welling up.

The general stood as if rooted to the spot, lost for words.

I've never heard of a skill so terrifying…

He looked up at the king and was shocked to see a chilling smile on the king's face.

From that day, the king changed, as if he'd become a different person.

From that day, the white-haired princess disappeared from sight.

The deaths at the temple were written off as an accident. A few days after, the king summoned ruffians with combat-related unique skills from all over the country to his castle.

"Bring me as many monsters as you can. The ones you can't capture, kill," he ordered.

He offered generous rewards, which the bunch of roughnecks greeted with joy. They became adventurers and set out to hunt monsters within the country and farther afield.

Nobody besides the knight general had an inkling that it was all part of the king's most horrific plan…

* * * *

One day, two years after the princess's disappearance, the king summoned the adventurers, whose levels had greatly increased since the beginning of the monster hunts. They gathered in the castle, eager to hear about an assignment he had for them, for which they were promised a year's wages.

The king surveyed the group of adventurers, pleased to see how much stronger they'd become in the last year.

"I have been informed that soldiers from a neighboring country are hiding out in a tower three villages to the north from here. They're plotting to attack us. Supposedly, they all have powerful combat unique skills. I would like you to kill every one of them."

The adventurers were astonished to be asked such a thing. Accustomed to fighting monsters, they thought some soldiers from a cowardly neighboring country that didn't dare proclaim open war would be only too easy to put down. Regardless, they set out for the tower at once.

The knight general watched them file out of the castle door with very mixed feelings.

*   *   *   *

It was very silent around the tower. Even though it was surrounded by a dense forest, there were no animals around. The adventurers, their senses sharpened through countless battles, felt the hair rise on the back of their necks as they approached the tower, surrounding it. They drew their weapons, and at the first sight of movement at the top of the tower, they uttered a battle cry and attacked.

A moment later, they were all dead, dissolving into light.

Even level-60 veterans died as soon as they entered the skill effect area, completely defenseless.

Shortly after, an arrow with a letter attached to it stuck into the wall next to one of the windows in the tower. As usual, the white-haired princess Vampia was happy to receive correspondence. She unrolled it at once.

"Leo, Father! You defeated the enemy soldiers! Thank goodness! I was so scared when I saw them," she said quietly to herself, her voice choked with tears.

A beautiful gemstone necklace glittered around her neck.

The princess had been told she'd contracted a serious contagious disease and had to live in seclusion until her recovery. The letters, sent to her by arrows, were her only means of contact with the outside world, her only source of joy. It heartened her to know that her father, the king, and Leo—who'd now become a royal guard—were keeping her safe. They killed the monsters that had come close to the tower, too. Vampia daydreamed of the day when she was cured and could stroll through the castle town together with Leo again.

The king had been looking after his daughter indeed—EXP from the adventurers and monsters she'd killed raised her level to 70. She was now stronger than the most illustrious knights in countries larger than theirs. After "feeding" the adventurers to her, the king decided it was time to make a move.

* * * *

Vampia woke up and went to the window to fetch that morning's letter.

"It's from Leo... What?! They found a cure?! It's in another country, and he'll take me there?! I can't believe it!"

She blushed at the thought of seeing Leo again after two years of living alone in the tower. The prospect of talking to him made her more excited than being cured of her illness, and she could think about nothing else for a while.

She worried she might disappoint him. While she'd been kept away from society for such a long time, he'd fulfilled his goal of becoming a royal knight and was probably doing lots of interesting things every day.

The only pretty dress she had in the tower was pure white, matching the color of her hair and skin. She quickly put it on and ran down the stairs, hurrying to a spot in the woods outside, as instructed. A carriage was waiting there for her. Leo stood beside it. He looked the same as she remembered, except that he was now wearing armor. His complexion didn't look very healthy, but he waved to her cheerfully.

"Leo! It's really you!"

"It's been so long. You're as pretty as ever."

Vampia was beside herself with joy. She stuck out her fist for a fist bump, but he just smiled awkwardly.

"What are you doing?" he asked.

"Oh... Nothing, sorry..."

He'd forgotten their special gesture of friendship. That took the wind out of Vampia's sails a bit, but Leo didn't seem to notice. He got into the carriage and motioned for her to come inside, too.

They rode for days, until the rhythm of the carriage shaking slightly on uneven roads became so familiar, they stopped noticing it. The coachman bought food for them, which Vampia shared with Leo. The journey was long, the carriage was cramped and dark, and the seats were hard, but Vampia didn't mind that at all. Her lonely life in the tower had been far, far worse. Being able to talk to Leo made every day on the road great.

A month later, the carriage stopped suddenly.

"Whoa!"

She was thrown off her seat, falling into Leo's arms. Her cheeks reddened, but she noticed something that disquieted her.

Why does he feel so cold?

Leo was cold to the touch. Since meeting him again, she'd been wondering if he was unwell, since his face was so pale, and now this?

Leo's expression was the same as usual when he spoke to her.

"Lou Vampia Cilrulis, I must offer you an apology. This will be my parting message."

"!"

His voice had changed. It was familiar, but it wasn't Leo's voice—it was the voice of an old man.

"There isn't much time left, so I will be brief. This boy, Leo, died on the day of your unique-skill announcement ceremony."

"What...?"

What he told her after was a profound shock for Vampia—that she'd been moved to the tower not because of an illness, but because of her unique skill. That the monsters and armed people who'd tried to attack the tower had all been sent by her father, and that it was her who'd killed them.

"Who are you...?" she managed in a hoarse voice.

The person she had taken for Leo was silent for a while.

"I am General Dullahan, the former captain head of the royal knights. I read the description of your skill that day…but that knowledge is strictly prohibited by the king."

Vampia remembered him—the strong yet kind general who'd watched over her when she lived at the castle.

"Why do you look like Leo?"

"I'm controlling his dead body with my unique skill, Revived Memory. The coachman and the horses are dead, too."

Vampia bit her lip. Leo was dead. That's why he looked as if he hadn't aged since the last time she saw him, why he didn't look well, why he felt cold to the touch, and why he didn't remember their friendship gesture. The letters that had been her lifeline were all probably written by General Dullahan, too.

She hung her head, shaking from anger. She tried to shut away her thoughts about Leo to curb her rising rage, which felt like darkness filling her chest.

"Why are you telling me this now?" she asked without emotion.

Leo's dead body looked her right in the eyes. "Because we're running out of time."

"What do you mean?"

"I cannot explain this to you now, Princess. I implore you not to return to Lendos. Don't let your father find you. There's money in this coach and a ring that can seal away your power. Please live the rest of your life in peace."

Vampia jumped from the carriage. The scenery outside was foreign to her. "Leo" continued talking, still sitting inside the carriage.

"Your unique skill is extremely powerful and dangerous. I don't want you, who played so innocently with the common-born children in town, to be made into a weapo—"

He stopped suddenly, becoming motionless. For a few moments, it was as if time had frozen, but then Leo's body, as well as the coachman and the horses, broke up into pixels and disappeared. Vampia tried to chase after the vanishing pixels, crying.

"No—no! Leo! Dullahan! Don't leave me! I have nowhere to go…!"

There was nobody left to answer her pleas.

At the back of the carriage, she found ten big gold coins (so much that five generations of commoners could live a life of leisure) and enough food to last her a lifetime. She moved them to her storage and walked away in a random direction, as there were no paths around, until she reached a town—it was Tonsa, in the country of Wagazud, a seedy place with high crime rates and abject poverty.

* * * *

Tonsa was the complete opposite of the peaceful town in Lendos where Vampia had grown up. She'd never seen such poverty before, with people dying of hunger in the streets. Everyone was desperate, and so theft and murder were commonplace. Never had she imagined that a place existed where parents would sell their young children into slavery.

"Eat as much as you want."

"Yes, thank you, miss!"

Vampia bought a small church, where she handed out free meals to orphans and slaves every day. Her church was the only ray of hope for the poor children born in the cruel environment of Tonsa.

Following Dullahan's advice, Vampia used the ring he gave her to block her unique skill's power from manifesting, living a quiet life out of trouble's way…but that was about to end.

"What…?"

She returned from shopping one day to find her church empty. The children who had so innocently played there just moments ago were gone, but not without a trace—there were tiny piles of items here and there among the broken furniture.

"No…"

All the children she'd been looking after had been killed, as she'd been informed by one of the men who'd surrounded her church. Grinning sadistically, they moved in to attack her, too. Tears rolled down Vampia's cheeks—tears of blood. She slipped off the special ring. Instantly, the whole town was dead.

Vampia stood up from the floor and smiled sorrowfully, surveying what had remained of the one safe shelter she'd created in Tonsa.

"Next time... Next time, it'll go better than this..."

After that, she traveled from one land to another. Wherever she arrived, she surrounded herself with children, but her happiness was always temporary. Sooner or later, someone would brutally end it. After annihilating seven countries, Vampia became convinced that all foreigners were evil, and she headed back to her homeland of Lendos, the place dearest to her heart.

It had been one year since she left the tower. Her level was 100. The tragedies that followed her wherever she went hurt her so deeply, broke her so much, that she forgot what Dullahan implored her not to do.

Back in her homeland after three years of absence, Vampia first went to the castle, her gait unsteady. The ring from Dullahan glittered on her finger as she entered the audience hall, where her father, the king, welcomed her with a tender embrace. Tears welled up in Vampia's eyes. She shut them, feeling as if she were melting, held by her father, taking in his warmth.

"Vampia, dear! You've returned to us!"

He seemed genuinely happy to see her. It had been so long since Vampia felt so relieved and joyous, too. Then she noticed the absence of her mother.

"Father, why is Mother not here?"

The captain of the royal knights was also nowhere in sight... He'd helped her with something, hadn't he? Wasn't he the one who'd helped her escape...? Her memories were hazy. She awaited her father's reply.

The king smiled, looking straight at her. "They're both dead, my dear."

"Mother and the captain?"

"Yes. Marid died in a sad accident. Dullahan was executed for treason a year ago."

Treason? What treason?

"I am General Dullahan, the former head of the royal knights. I read

the description of your skill that day…but that knowledge is strictly prohibited by the king."

"We're running out of time."

"I implore you not to return to Lendos. Don't let your father find you. There's money in this coach and a ring that can seal away your power. Please live the rest of your life in peace."

"Your unique skill is extremely powerful and dangerous. I don't want you, who played so innocently with the common-born children in town, to be made into a weapo—"

Memories of what Dullahan had told her that time after helping her escape came flooding back. He'd been executed for treason, for opposing something her father had been planning…for helping her escape?

"Why was he executed?"

"My sweet, sweet daughter, I will tell you everything as a last favor."

The king raised his hand, holding a beautiful jewel in it. He looked down at his daughter with a merciful smile.

"You have an extraordinary power. Just as I'd planned, you managed to single-handedly destroy all our neighboring countries. The only thing I had to do was hire some bandits to ensure everything would be on track."

She understood then. The tragedies that seemed to follow her, the murders of the children she tried to protect, Dullahan's execution—her father had orchestrated it all. He'd manipulated her into using her unique skill to destroy the neighboring countries in order to effortlessly expand Lendos's territory.

"It started with your lie about me being ill…"

"Oh, but your power is like a plague; it is truly catastrophic. You escaped from the tower where I kept you, but I always knew exactly where you were, thanks to that gemstone necklace."

Her father gave her that necklace as a birthday gift when she was actually ill and so unwell, she had to stay in bed. The gemstone was paired with the one the king had.

"Unfortunately, my dear, you've grown too powerful. Nobody in our kingdom comes close. Of course, I knew this was bound to happen when I set the plan in motion. My dear daughter, may you rest in peace."

Before Vampia could take her ring off, the king shattered the gemstone in his hand. Its twin gemstone in Vampia's necklace burst into pieces...and so did Vampia's body.

"The magical power she had amassed through three years of killing is finally getting released. Even a level-hundred monstrosity, the most powerful the world has ever known, can be vanquished in a moment," the king remarked flatly, watching the afterimage of his daughter fade away.

Vampia's funeral was held with due ceremony, and she was buried next to her mother within the castle grounds. Over the next few years, Lendos absorbed all the vacant neighboring land into its territory, becoming the greatest country in the world.

One night, the soldiers patrolling the grounds of the oldest castle in the Great Kingdom of Lendos saw a ghostly figure of a beautiful girl in the castle courtyard. Her hair and skin were almost translucent. She wore a snow-white dress, and on her head were horns growing in a circle like a crown.

"What's a little girl doing out here in the middle of the night?"

"Huh. She's eerily pretty..."

"Wait, I think I've seen her somewhere before?"

The two soldiers dissolved into nothingness. The beautiful girl kept on walking to her birthplace, to her resting place. Her passage brought with it death. It was as if she were surrounded by a gigantic dome in which no life was allowed. People of all ages died instantly when she got near.

She arrived in the audience hall. The king fearfully hid behind his last remaining guard.

"You can't be alive! You monster!"

Vampia had returned from the grave. She didn't know why. All she felt was a great hunger and depression. She reached toward her father and stroked his cheek, hoping to find something that would fill the void in her heart. Both her father and his last royal guard melted away. There was no one left alive in the castle.

Vampia headed over to her grave. There were two names on the headstone—Marid Cilrulis, and Lou Vampia Cilrulis.

"'Vampia'...?" The girl read out the name quietly.

It sounded familiar, but she wasn't sure why. She traced the letters with her finger before leaving the castle graveyard.

For the next few decades, she wandered all over the continent, extinguishing countless lives, as if that was her sole purpose. She left behind a desolate landscape of ruins, of land entirely barren. It became populated only by those unfortunate enough to revive as undead.

"Leo..."

The girl remembered a boy's name, but not what he looked like. She repeated his name every now and again, so as not to forget that one last memory dear to her.

Several more decades passed, and those decades turned into centuries.

*　*　*　*

The girl craved release from her existence. She couldn't think of a single reason to keep on living. The undead were closer to death than anyone, but at the same time, they were the furthest from it. The girl was an undead, and so she couldn't die. Buildings had fallen apart into piles of rubble, and the piles of rubble had crumbled to dust when the girl met someone.

"Oh, hello."

His hood concealed his face, but his voice sounded young. The girl was surprised, and joyous even, to encounter a living being after thousands of years with only undead for company. But she found herself overcome with the urge to kill.

He can't be an ordinary human, coming here alone...

She approached him, and to her great confusion, he remained standing.

"Looks like I'm immune to your power." He shrugged, amused.

"Impossible...," she said.

She was level 120. Only an undead, for whom death was impossible, could survive her killing ability. Yet she could sense that this was a human, not an undead.

The man laughed as if she was being funny. "Sorry, sorry. I'm an admin of this world, so skills like that don't work on me."

"A world admin? Do you mean you're a god?"

"No, but close, I guess?"

He shrugged nonchalantly. Then he pointed up, as if he was about to tell her something very important.

"The mother to us all entrusted me with selecting a world that met certain criteria set out by her. I've been visiting countless worlds before this one. Will it surprise you to hear there are so many others just like yours?"

"..."

"From your point of view, this world is everything there is, but to our Great Mother, it's fairly inconsequential. A little bubble that she wouldn't notice bursting."

The man pointed to her.

"Anyway, back to what I came here to talk about. There's nobody in this world capable of killing you, but your existence makes it impossible for this world to thrive and evolve. Which is why I've come all this way to end your world."

She smiled. In the light of what he'd just said, the man found that charming smile rather chilling.

"Ah. So your task is to pop the bubbles of the unwanted worlds," she replied.

Her smile looked more as if someone had cut the corner of her mouth to widen it, her eyes like those of a corpse. And yet they brimmed with tears as she fell on her knees, lifting her gaze to the sky.

"At last... At last, this hell will end! What are you waiting for? Please end it already!"

For well over a thousand years, she'd been aimlessly roaming the empty land, tortured by her ceaseless hunger, driven to madness by her immortality. Her world ending, her life ending—that would be the sweetest relief.

The man cocked his head at her and uttered a short laugh. "Sorry, but I'm not going to erase you."

She attacked him.

"What mockery is this?! Kill me! Kill me! Kill me already! I want to die!!!" she shouted, taking a mighty swing at him with a giant ax.

Before the blade could strike him, it suddenly froze in the air, and mysterious text appeared in the air:

System block

"Our Great Mother did instruct me to destroy the inhabitants of the failed worlds along with their land, but I'm making my own decisions now. I will keep you in custody until the right time comes."

He held out his hand, and a pitch-black hole opened underneath it. It began pulling at the girl like a powerful whirlpool, but she would not budge. The man was surprised.

"Wow, you can resist that? I should've figured. You're the queen of this world, after all."

"You want to trap me? I don't want it! I don't want to be kept in confinement yet again!"

She remembered being imprisoned in a tower when she was still human. Forced by lies to stay in that cramped space all alone, daydreaming of being with her best friend again someday, unaware that he was already dead.

"Don't worry, you won't be alone. I'm planning on keeping five... no, six entities like you in there."

She glared at him fiercely.

"Sorry," he said, his tone suddenly turning very matter-of-fact, "I don't have much time; explaining everything to you would take too long. I hope for great stuff from you!"

The girl felt her consciousness being swallowed up by darkness.

When she came to, she was in a strange castle. As the man promised, she met five others like her in there and realized that some great force had trapped them all.

She tried to kill the others and couldn't. But neither could they kill her. Hundreds of years passed by without anything happening…until that fateful day.

*   *   *   *

The girl had been vacantly staring out of a window at the empty sky, when she noticed something lying on the ground.

A human? Impossible. I haven't seen a single human here in centuries…

The person stood up and looked at some point in front of him. Profoundly shaken, he fell to his knees. He reminded her of someone from a long, long time ago.

She couldn't resist the urge to call out to him.

"You there."

For some reason, she was filled with anticipation.

"How did you get here—?"

"Oh… What are we going to do?! We can't— We can't log out!"

She gasped when he put his hands on her shoulders. It'd been forever since she'd felt the warmth of a living human. He wasn't cold, like the other boy… He wasn't just a lie. He was a real human…but then why didn't her unique skill kill him? She was shocked and confused.

Who is he…?

She didn't know what to do with this strange person who'd appeared out of nowhere. While he was unconscious again, the other Evil Overlords also tried to kill him, to no effect. They couldn't even scratch him.

When she was later told that this boy had become their master, it triggered her most traumatic memories, and she reacted with fury. Later, when she learned that the boy's death would also mean the death of every one of his minions, she felt hopeful again for the first time in centuries. He was good news after all.

Character Designs

Player:

SHUUTAROU

A thirteen-year-old with a friendly smile and beige hair. Plays a swordfighter. Uses beginners' equipment in the first half of Chapter 01: a generic leather breastplate, white linen clothes, dark-brown boots, and a basic sword. Upon his return to Allistras, he dons high-spec armor with a semitransparent Fang Sword made for him by the Evil Overlord Theodore.

Mob:

PUNIO

The first monster Shuutarou summoned to his dungeon. Started out as a regular slime, but after being fed all of Ross Maora's prisoners as EXP, it achieved its ultimate form as a sinister black Abyss Slime.

Boss Mob:

ELROAD <<THE FIRST EVIL OVERLORD>>

A handsome man with blue hair and red eyes who dresses like a butler. Very polite manner of speech and always reading difficult books. Has his hands full trying to keep the motley Evil Overlord crew in check.

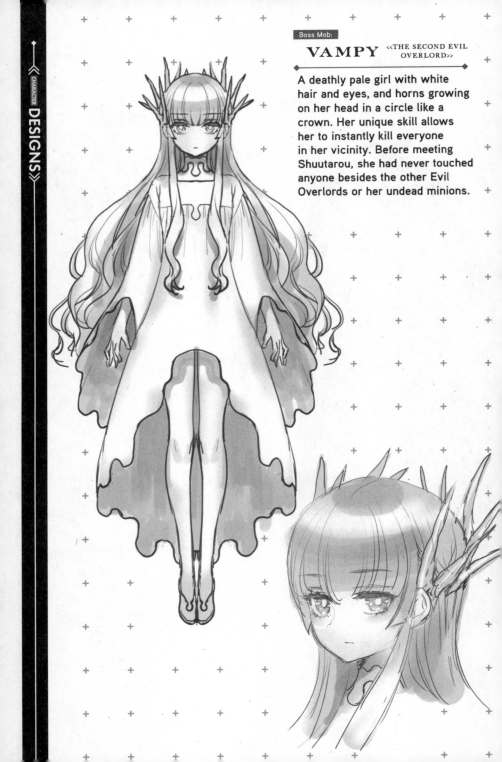

Boss Mob:

VAMPY «THE SECOND EVIL OVERLORD»

A deathly pale girl with white hair and eyes, and horns growing on her head in a circle like a crown. Her unique skill allows her to instantly kill everyone in her vicinity. Before meeting Shuutarou, she had never touched anyone besides the other Evil Overlords or her undead minions.

Boss Mob:

GALLARUS «THE THIRD EVIL OVERLORD»

A redheaded, bearded giant with an imposing physique. Constantly training to become even stronger. Has been eagerly waiting for the opportunity to go out into the world and expand his dominion.

Beard A

190

152

Mark on her back

Boss Mob:

SYLVIA 《THE FOURTH EVIL OVERLORD》

A beautiful woman with gorgeous, long silver hair and beast-like blue eyes. Appears coolheaded at a glance but is a firm believer in the survival of the fittest.

Boss Mob:

THEODORE <<THE FIFTH EVIL OVERLORD>>

A swordfighter with a black cape, wiry black hair, and golden eyes. Taciturn and always serious. A perfectionist who's as demanding of others as he is of himself, tirelessly seeking to improve. Makes his own armor and weapons.

Boss Mob:

BERTRAND ‹‹THE SIXTH EVIL OVERLORD››

Lord of the elves, a race on the brink of dying
out. Comes off as carefree, but he's actually
more deliberate in his actions than people give
him credit for. Unlike the other Evil Overlords,
he's more pragmatic about his powers.

Thank you so much for buying *The Unimplemented Overlords Have Joined the Party!*

What propelled me to write this novel was the fact that the genre of stories about players getting trapped in VR games where dying in the game meant dying for real all but dried up on Shousetsuka ni Narou, the website where I post my writings. It used to be a very popular genre, especially the series featuring a certain black-haired knight or the one about a certain player terrified of dying, but nowadays, most plotlines about VR games don't feature the *Death is for real* or *Players can't leave the game* tropes anymore, which I personally loved for the drama. So I thought I'd throw my own little kindling on this dying fire in the hope that more writers would follow suit.

I wrote this as a multi-POV story. In the first volume, we have three protagonists: Shuutarou, Misaki, and Wataru.

Misaki's arc is about the struggle of a powerless, ordinary player.

Wataru faces different problems as a strong player who tries to lead others.

* * *

Shuutarou is a lucky exception. Writing too much from his perspective would take away from the tension of the *Trapped in the game and death is for real* genre that I so enjoy, but it was quite hard for me to decide what was too much. Sorry if I gave you the impression the story would be about Shuutarou going around mowing down hordes of enemies together with his boss mob friends.

As for the six Evil Overlords, I spent a lot of time deciding what each would look like, what their personality would be, and how strong they'd be. I actually created them for another story and had a heap of reference materials for them already. (All lost due to accidentally resetting my iPhone…) Originally, they were to be ruled by a ruthless guy with unmatched strength, but for this story, I made Shuutarou their master.

Putting a weak child in charge of the Evil Overlords enabled me to give the story a more human angle instead of it being about evil villains.

Kawaku's illustrations breathed life into Shuutarou, Misaki, Wataru, and my Evil Overlords. Elroad's and Bertrand's designs gave me goose bumps—they were exactly how I pictured them in my head. Amazing.

The story was originally published online; this is a more polished, expanded version with added illustrations. I hope you liked it! Depending on how it sells, I might be able to publish Volumes 2 and 3 alongside a story taking a very different trajectory from what I made available online! Fingers crossed lots of readers kindly buy my book!

Last but not least, the third volume of my debut series, *Frontier World*, is out, courtesy of Famitsu Bunko. It's a laid-back story about a

VR game, without the *Death is for real* element. Check it out if you're a fan of the genre!

And this concludes my afterword.

Thank you again for buying my novel!

Let's meet again, shall we?

Nagawasabi64
November 30, 2020

HELLO, I'M KAWAKU, THE ILLUSTRATOR. THIS STORY FEATURES A LOT OF CHARACTERS, AND IT'S BEEN MY GREAT PLEASURE TO DESIGN THEM. I HOPE EVERYONE FINDS AT LEAST ONE CHARACTER THEY'RE FOND OF!